STALKED BY A HELL PACK OF VAMPIRE DOGS

Michael Drake had hidden the truth from everyone—his wife, his children, his neighbors. Why unearth the secrets of the past?

Why reveal his real family name was not Drake but Dracula?

But now as he stared in the moonlight at the huge German shepherd who was the favorite of all his pet dogs, he saw a creature he had never known—its massive jaws open and slavering, a macabre green light shining from its gleaming, hypnotic eyes, its every muscle taut as it led the pack that closed in on Michael and his loved ones.

And suddenly Michael recognized the horror that was his terrifying heritage. Not even he was safe from—

HOUNDS OF DRACULA

Big Bestsellers from SIGNET

HOUNDS OF DRACULA

A novel by
Ken Johnson

From a screenplay by Frank Ray Perilli

A SIGNET BOOK
NEW AMERICAN LIBRARY
TIMES MIRROR

COPYRIGHT © 1977 BY FRANK RAY PERILLI

First published in Great Britain by Everest Books, Ltd., 1977

 SIGNET TRADEMARK REG. U.S. PAT. OFF. AND FOREIGN COUNTRIES
REGISTERED TRADEMARK—MARCA REGISTRADA
HECHO EN CHICAGO, U.S.A.

SIGNET, SIGNET CLASSICS, MENTOR, PLUME AND MERIDIAN BOOKS
are published by The New American Library, Inc.,
1301 Avenue of the Americas, New York, New York 10019

FIRST SIGNET PRINTING, OCTOBER, 1977

1 2 3 4 5 6 7 8 9

PRINTED IN THE UNITED STATES OF AMERICA

Do you really laugh at dreams,
black magic, miracles, nocturnal
vampires and Thessalian prophecy?
>   —Horace, *Epistularum* II,
>   ii, 209-210.

I believe in . . . the resurrection
of the flesh . . .
>   —part of the Creed,
>   attributed to St. Jude
>   by St. Augustine

If ever there was in the world
a warranted and proven history,
it is that of vampires: nothing
is lacking, official reports,
testimonials of persons of standing,
of surgeons, of clergymen, of
judges, the judicial evidence is
all-embracing.
>   —Jean Jacques Rousseau

I found out, however, that Transylvania is real—a province that belonged to Hungary for almost a thousand years and that now is part of modern Romania. In Stoker's novel there were some fairly detailed descriptions of the towns of Cluj and Bistrita, and the Borgo Pass in the Carpathian Mountains. These, too, proved real. If all that geographical data is genuine, I reasoned, why not Dracula himself?

—Raymond T. McNally and Radu
  Florescu, *In Search of Dracula*
  (Warner Books, 1973)

ONE:

Tomb of the Draculas

Private Laszlo Vukanovic watched the watery yellow sun preparing to dip behind the craggy outlines of the mountains. He shivered involuntarily, despite his warm buttoned-up leaf-green tunic and his shin-high black leather boots. Far below to the west lay the flat plain of the fertile, well-cultivated valley, dotted with a surprisingly wide variety of color—conifers, weeping birch, plum, apple, cherry and pear trees and

1

their blossoms, whose petals spangled the grass beneath them. It was natural, pleasant, even beautiful territory. And yet, as dusk approached and the fading sun began to turn the towering steeps of the Carpathians a pale rose color, Laszlo felt instinctively that something of the daytime warmth and wholesomeness went too suddenly out of the countryside. The starkness of the barren upper reaches of the mountains—Carpathians to the east, Transylvanian Alps to the south— quickly and ominously asserted themselves as the colors of field and tree, blossom and fruit faded, diluted by the monotone of twilight.

He looked at his watch. They'd be finished soon. Only a few more charges to go. From the clump of bushes behind which he stood he could see the small knot of men, crouched over their radios and instrument panels—the rows of buttons which would set off the charges.

For three days now, they had been bivouacked out here in the foothills of the mountains on training maneuvers—target practice, assault courses and testing light to medium explosives.

Laszlo was idly scanning the bony, finger-like crags of the mountains, now in silhouette, once again. No wonder it was so quiet all the time, he mused. No bird or animal in its right mind would want to inhabit such a joyless, foreboding region. Not after nightfall, at any rate.

The thought had barely flickered through his mind when the explosion went off. He felt the shock wave first, like a sharp blow to his rib cage and stomach muscles, then the deafening blast boomed out, rumbling away in echoes, off the mountains and down to the plain below. The earth beneath his feet shook like a minor earth tremor and a gigantic billow of dark-brown smoke rose slowly in a pall, far ahead of the group of men in front of him.

He stepped out of cover, trotting the few yards to the detonation squad, hefting the strap of his rifle over his right shoulder as he came to a halt beside Captain Gheorghita. The captain was staring intently toward the site of the explosion through his heavy-duty binoculars. Tiny figures were already on the scene, gesticulating back toward the officer. After a few moments the captain lowered the glasses and raised his walkie-talkie unit to his lips. The voice of another man at a detonation unit positioned farther down the valley to the west crackled over the radio in acknowledgment. At first, Laszlo thought Captain Gheorghita was about to give the order for another charge to be detonated, but instead, the officer barked out sharply:

"Stop! They have found . . . something. Something they want us to look at. All units . . . that's it for today. No further blasting.

Sergeant Ociscisc will take over from now on. Over and out."

The captain let his radio dangle on its strap at his side, then turned to Laszlo and the men crouching by the detonator panel.

"You, you and you. Come with me," he ordered, and Laszlo and two of the other soldiers fell in behind him as he jogged toward the explosion site. Above it, the dark pall of smoke hung in the air like a miniature storm cloud, dispersing only gradually at its edges.

Within a few minutes the captain and his men arrived at the scene. Another officer and a group of four soldiers stood peering into a deep, narrow chasm in the earth. Its steep sides were flanked by uniform blocks of masonry, and a row of granite steps led down into impenetrable darkness. One of the soldiers began to hand out protective hard-hats from a backpack he had been carrying on his shoulders. The second officer flicked on a powerful flashlight and aimed it down the fissure. Fascinated, officers and men continued to peer into the opening as they put on their protective headgear. But dust was still rising in clouds from the depths, and the flashlight picked out only a long, tapering cone of light in which danced swirling dark particles.

"What is it—a cave?" one of the soldiers asked no one in particular.

"Whatever it is, it was man-made," Captain

Gheorghita said. "Look at those walls. That's no natural fissure."

His fellow officer continued to play the torch around the descending walls of the passage.

"Well," said Gheorghita, "no point waiting around. Let's go."

Flicking on his own flashlight, he led the way slowly down the flight of stairs. The men followed, backed up by the second captain. By now the dust was beginning to settle, and at the foot of the stairs, Captain Gheorghita flicked his light around the interior of what appeared to be a chamber, hewn from the natural rock. Unlike the smoothly faced walls of the narrow stairway, the chamber's walls were rough and unfinished, and the footsteps of the men descending echoed eerily around its uneven contours. There were large lumps of debris, obviously fallen from the walls and ceiling, strewn about the floor. The captain and the rest of the men moved slowly into the excavation. Gheorghita played his high-beam torch on the farthest wall and noticed that it was smoothly finished. Along this were what appeared to be square-shaped plaques bearing some type of inscriptions. There were three parallel rows of them.

Captain Gheorghita went toward the wall, carefully negotiating the fallen rocks, and began to wipe the dust away from one of the plaques with a gloved hand. When the miniature dust storm that this caused had cleared, his flashlight beam picked out, carefully carved into the stone square by an experienced mason's chisel, the following inscription:

COUNT IGOR DRACULA
1601–1670

As he studied it, his fellow officer, Captain Thurzo, who had moved to the front of the small gathering of men, wiped clean another of the square plaques. It read:

COUNT MIKHAIL DRACULA
1670–1735

It was obviously a family crypt. The flashlight beams of the soldiers picked out more of the *in memoriam* inscriptions—the wall was dotted with them in three neat horizontal rows of four plaques each, twelve in all: BARONESS EVA DRACULA, 1701–1763, COUNT FREDERIC DRACULA, 1775–1815, and so on.

Captain Gheorghita turned to face the men, who were gazing curiously at the inscriptions on the wall of this strange, remote sepulcher.

"Otescu," he said. "Report to Sergeant Ociscisc: all blasting operations in this area to be suspended immediately. On the double!"

"Yes, sir!"

"And tell him to notify headquarters—we need an archaeologist."

"Very well, sir."

Private Otescu saluted, wheeled and made for the steps leading up into the gathering twilight outside. Captain Thurzo turned to Laszlo, who was still fascinatedly studying the wall's roll of the dead of a century and more ago.

"You," the captain said. "Stand guard overnight."

"Yes, sir," Laszlo said, saluting. He looked quickly over at Captain Gheorghita, half-hoping that the other officer would withdraw Thurzo's order in favor of some other duty, but he could not think why the captain should do so. The captain simply nodded at Thurzo and, extending an arm, indicated the way out to the other men, playing his flashlight over the floor so that they would not stumble.

Captain Thurzo handed Laszlo his flashlight, patted his shoulder, saluted and turned to follow the others. Soon their footsteps faded up the stone staircase and Laszlo was left alone with his thoughts, the twelve ancient sarcophagi . . . and the night.

Whether or not there is a living Dracula in our midst it is an accepted historical and medical fact that vampirism has existed throughout the centuries.

> —Christopher Lee, in an introduc-
> tion to a comic-book version of
> *Dracula* (Ballantine Books, Inc.,
> 1966)

Even Dracula is to be pitied in a way. All people who do dreadful things are to be pitied. I have used a phrase—the Loneli-ness of Evil—many times, and I believe it is true.

> —Christopher Lee, in an interview
> with the author, October 1967

TWO:

Night's Black Agent

By 11:45 p.m. Laszlo's vaguely lurking un-easiness about being left alone in a dank, shadowy, subterranean tomb had left him, only to be replaced by another more rational, yet equally undesirable mood: boredom. For the first few hours he had sat or stood by the staircase that led up into the Transylvanian countryside, a district plunged unpleasantly into darkness, it was true, but it seemed a much more wholesome place to be than down in the bowels of the earth with the remains of the long dead. Each time a tiny loose fragment of chipped stone dropped from the walls or ceiling of the chamber, loosened by the earlier explosion and released perhaps by the gradual shifting of the fractured rock strata above, Laszlo had been tempted to run for his life up the stone steps. Each falling fragment sounded like thunder in the hollow, echoing, claustrophobic chamber. At the slightest noise, he had repeatedly grabbed his rifle, or darted the beam of his flashlight trembling over every inch of the walls, ceiling and floors.

But eventually, he had begun to laugh inwardly at his unfounded nervousness, his groundless fears. Those were the fears of superstitious country folk, peasants—not of a mature young soldier raised in the bustle of modern Bucharest. Those people whose names decorated the plaques on the wall— whoever they had been—had been dead for a hundred years, most of them even longer. They couldn't harm anyone. The rest of the rockbound cell was empty, save for the dust and debris. There wasn't so much as a rat or a spider in the place. So what was there to be afraid of? That, at least, was how he gradually reasoned with himself, reassuringly.

By 9:30 he had become bold and taken

off his **protective** helmet. A quarter-hour later and he **was sitting** on the floor, his back propped **against** the side of the staircase, rifle leaning **beside** him as he idly smoked a cigarette. At 10:00 p.m. he had snapped on his transistor radio and was listening to its tinny two-inch speaker bouncing Gypsy guitar and violin music off the walls. But even that became a bore after forty-five minutes or more, and, impatiently, he flicked off the switch.

He looked at his watch again. It was approaching midnight. The minutes, let alone the hours, seemed to be grinding by. Maybe they would relieve him soon. . . .

He stubbed out yet another cigarette, counted how many he had left in his pack and worked out how long they would last him if he were left on guard until morning. Then he remembered: it *would* be until morning. Overnight, Captain Thurzo had said. Stand guard overnight. He sighed frustratedly. Stand guard against what? Who but an imbecile would want to come here in the middle of the night? And besides, until today, the vault had been totally hidden to anyone in the outside world for a century or more. At least since the last occupant's remains had been placed there.

God! If only he had someone to talk to, or even a flask of coffee or a bottle of wine.

He got to his feet, threw back his head and yawned, flexing his shoulders and arms

10

and standing up on his toes. Idly, he picked up his flashlight and ambled toward the stairs. He looked up at the narrow oblong of stars that could be dimly discerned at the top of the ascending passage and began to climb upward. Outside, he listened to the sounds of nocturnal insects making their regular, rhythmic calls and answers. Somewhere off in the distance an owl hooted. As his eyes became used to the darkness, he was gradually able to pick out the clusters of trees and the shoulders of the mountains, edged with silver from the moon. He glanced up. A full moon. The night air was crisp, turning chill. Laszlo shivered slightly, turned up the collar of his uniform, flicked on his flashlight and went back down into the underground sepulcher.

As he languidly settled down into a semi-crouching position by the side of the flight of stone steps, Laszlo began to think over his situation. Here he was in an ancient, uncomfortable tomb, underground, in the god-forsaken reaches of the Carpathian mountains, when he could have been at home in Bucharest, enjoying a night out. He thought of Ilona. He ran a hand through his curly, short-cropped black hair and sighed inwardly. Had he been wise in joining the army? Ilona, back home there in Bucharest, no doubt by now curled up in her warm bed . . . or even out with some other lucky young guy . . . no, she wouldn't. She said so in her letters. Back there . . . He frowned. Of course, it was all very well thinking fondly of Ilona and "back there." But in reality, "back there" there was no work for him, nothing for an unskilled man, at any rate. Which was why he had joined the army in the first place, to learn some skill, a trade. Sure, it had been exciting, going out in the field, on maneuvers, learning to shoot, unarmed combat, survival courses and so on. But what had he really learned so far that would be of any use to him in later life? He looked at his surroundings and shrugged sarcastically. How to become a cemetery superintendent, perhaps?

Without thinking, he reached in his tunic pocket for another cigarette, but just as he was about to take out the pack, something made him pause and listen. Beneath him, somewhere in the earth nearby, he sensed a deep rumbling, distant at first, but growing louder. Trickles of dust began to trail down from various points in the ceiling of the chamber. He grabbed his torch and swept it around. The rumbling *was* growing closer—some kind of aftereffect of the explosion, perhaps. Small fragments of rock began to tumble down from the ceiling and walls. Laszlo got to his feet. A large chunk of rock fell, then more dust, then more rocks. He made for the steps.

By now the whole tomb seemed to be shaking gently on its natural foundations and clouds of dust cascaded down from the ceiling, choking the air. Amid the dull thuds of the occasional falling rocks, Laszlo heard a different sound, a kind of nerve-jarring, grating sound of stone upon stone, as if something heavy were grinding against something equally solid.

Then, as quickly as it had started, the tremor subsided and the minor rockslide from the walls and ceiling ceased. Laszlo, halfway up the stone stairway, paused and peered back down into the chamber. His flashlight played on a solid curtain of dust hanging in the air. No . . . it was definitely over, no more rocks were falling, not even tiny fragments. Only the pall of dust particles, drifting gradually to the floor.

It *must* have been the strata settling again, fissures shoring up against each other; earth fractures that the detonation had opened and weakened. Laszlo wheeled and slowly, carefully, picked his way down the steps again, still playing the beam of his flashlight around. He stood at the foot of the steps waiting, and it was several minutes before the dust settled sufficiently for him to see even a few feet. More rock debris now littered the floor of the chamber, but beyond, toward the wall of stone plaques, he could faintly discern a larger, dark shape. He stepped forward gingerly, putting his feet

13

down carefully as he moved through the jumble of jagged fallen rock. His flashlight stabbed through the gloom to reveal a gray oblong shape, jutting out of the wall like a drawer left three-quarters open, except that this "drawer" had a lid. The front end, nearest to him, was formed by one of the square stone plaques.

A coffin! One of the large sarcophagi had been dislodged from its rack in the wall. Slowly, he edged toward it. Strange . . . this one bore no inscription. No one seemed to have noticed it earlier. Still, soldiers were not archaeologists; they were not expected to make a full examination of the crypt and its contents, they were simply to stand by until the experts arrived.

Suddenly, he froze. It was moving! The great gray oblong object was still gradually slipping out of its aperture a few inches at a time at irregular intervals, making the nerve-grating sound he had heard moments ago during the disturbance. *It was almost as if some unseen force were thrusting it out of the wall.*

Laszlo wanted to turn on his heel and run, but something prevented him. He stood, mesmerized almost, watching as the huge sarcophagus edged farther and farther out of the wall until, at last, it fell with a deafening boom to the floor of the vault, raising a small dust cloud as it did so.

He stared at it curiously, with all the fatal fascination of an animal transfixed in the headlamps of a car. It did not move again. Recovering himself a little, he quickly flashed his torch nervously over the other coffins in the wall. None of them appeared to have moved. Laszlo turned his attention back to the fallen casket. Of course . . . it must have been dislodged by the after-tremor, and the slight tilting of the chamber must have caused it to slip out gradually. The sepulcher was silent once more, save for his own breathing, which he was restraining with some effort.

What should he do? Report the matter? To do that he would have to desert his post. And the camp was a good three-quarters of a mile away. No . . . he'd simply have to wait.

He gazed fascinatedly at the large gray sarcophagus. He wondered who was inside and what he would look like after all the decades. He had seen only one corpse before —of his father. What would it look like? How many years? There was no way of telling. Of all the coffins in the underground vault, this one bore no inscription, no indication at all of its age, or its occupant's identity. He glanced at the square, gaping black hole that it had occupied a few minutes previously, then back at the coffin again.

Supposing he took a look inside . . . no one would know. The lid might have broken open as the heavy object fell from its niche in the wall. Yes, he could tell them that. It wouldn't do any harm.

Slowly, he moved toward it. He knelt and ran his hands along the lid, examining the edge for clasps or locks. It did not seem to have any. He grasped the edges of the lid and tugged. It moved slightly. He tugged again. More movement. A third effort, and the whole lid lifted off in his hands. Keeping his eyes on the interior of the casket, trying to see what lay inside, he placed the lid on the floor beside it.

There in the oblong box lay a jumble of white cloth; grave cerements . . . the shroud. There did not even appear to be a form beneath the cloth, as if its former owner had already crumbled to dust. The only unusual feature of the contents was a round wooden dowel, thicker than a man's wrist, sticking up vertically from the center of the bundled-up folds of dusty white linen. Gingerly, Laszlo took hold of it with one hand, testing it. It appeared to be firmly fixed into something beneath the shroud. He put his other hand around the wooden rod also and began to twist it backward and forward. Then he tugged upward. It was jammed in fairly solidly. Bracing himself and with some effort, twisting and pulling upward at the same time, he gradually managed to extract the wooden stake. He stood up, still holding it in both hands, looking at it. The end had been whittled to a sharp point and was stained a dark, rusty color. Out of the corner of his eye, he suddenly detected a faint movement. He looked down into the coffin. The folds of the shroud seemed to be moving. He could not believe the evidence of his own eyes and stood there, staring. His first, split-second rationalization of the phenomenon was that perhaps the linen was merely settling back into place after his efforts in yanking out the wooden rod, whatever it was. But no . . . wait . . .

Laszlo's eyes widened with terror as he saw quite definitely that the shroud was not settling, but filling out! Riveted with fear, he dazedly dropped the wooden stake to the floor as the realization dawned upon him: something was taking shape beneath the winding sheet!

An odor reached his nostrils; a strange, fetid smell, peculiarly alien and yet, in some indefinable way, oddly familiar. He had smelled it only once before, but could not remember when or where. *It was the unique, sweet, sour, sickly stench of death!*

Like an automaton, his eyes still fixed on the thing in the casket, the white, slowly writhing something under the cloth, Laszlo cautiously took a step backward, then another. The object within the coffin was growing larger and larger by the second, the shroud moving more and more agitatedly, and yet . . . *whatever it was that was taking shape beneath that musty linen was not of human form.*

Laszlo's heart pounded so wildly and loudly it felt as if it were about to burst out through his rib cage. His eyes bulged from their sockets in stark terror and his face and body were coated with a film of cold perspiration. He could barely feel his legs as, instinctively, tremblingly, they slowly backed him away from the nightmarish tableau unfolding before him. He wanted to cry out, to scream for help, but the muscles of his throat were constricted, his vocal cords locked in some stubborn paralysis, born of utter fear. He tried to steel himself to force a deafening cry. His breath came in short, irregular gasps and gulps, like that of a person in severe shock. With one titanic effort, he forced himself to draw in a mighty, lung-wracking gasp of air.

Laszlo Vukanovic never knew whether or not he managed that gargantuan scream. For at that moment a huge, hellish dark shape flashed up from the coffin before him, seeming to fly through the air like a pouncing black panther. As it did so, it uttered the most blood-curdling, ear-splitting roar of fury, and within a split second, it was upon him. The last thing he remembered was the hot, fetid stench of the creature's breath blasting into his face, its massive weight crashing upon him and pinioning him to the rough floor of the tomb and two rapid rapier-like stabs simultaneously in the side of his neck. And all the while, somewhere away in the background, he could hear the sound of a human voice; a human voice in utter torment, screaming and howling like a madman in sheer terror and agony. It was his own.

I felt a warm rasping at my throat, then came a consciousness of the awful truth, which chilled me to the heart and sent the blood surging up through my brain. Some great animal was lying on me and now licking my throat . . . Through my eyelashes I saw above me the two great flaming eyes of a gigantic wolf. Its sharp white teeth gleamed in the gaping red mouth, and I could feel its hot breath fierce and acrid upon me.

—Bram Stoker, *Dracula's Guest*
(1914)

THREE:

When Graves Give Up Their Dead

For several minutes the gigantic gray-black shape crouched over the slumped, inert body of the young soldier, its jaws clamped like a vise upon his torn jugular vein. The sound of excited, snorting canine greed rasped, echoing from the walls of the vault, accompanied by the hideous lapping and gurgling of human blood.

At length, the creature lifted its head, letting the limp, rag-doll torso of Laszlo slump disjointedly back to the ground. Its ears rose up, satanic and pointed. Its eyes blazed with an unnatural greenish light. Its enormous jaws, flanked on either side by abnormally huge canine fangs, were drenched in blood that dripped in great gobs to the dusty floor, as a great swathe of a tongue lashed obscenely from side to side with relish.

A hound from hell itself had returned . . . and was now satiated, renewed with warm, youthful blood.

For a moment more, the monstrous beast stood there, towering over the lifeless bundle of army green that had been its prey. Then it began to gaze around the tomb, sniffing the air with its great snout. It turned and surveyed the fallen sarcophagus from which it had launched itself upon its victim, then shifted its muscular body around to observe the row of inscribed wall plaques which hid the rest of the entombed undead of the Dracula brood.

The hound strode over to the first vertical row of three plaques and, standing on its hind legs, began to claw and sniff at the uppermost, the one whose inscription announced that it contained the unearthly remains of Count Igor Dracula. With a paw the size of a child's head, the brute pawed anxiously at the edges of the plaque, then, with an impatient whine, dropped down on all fours again. It stood stock still, attentively, for a while, as if by some supernatural means it were recalling something deep in the dark recesses of its vulpine brain . . . remembering sounds, smells and images of a life before . . . two centuries or more ago. . . .

Once more its eyes took on an eerie, preternatural greenish glint, as the misty images came wreathing back, blurred at first, but slowly sharpening in the mind's eye of its gargantuan, satanic skull. . . .

Veidt Smit, stablemaster to the wealthy Krymlac family, onetime heirs to the Turk-conquering Szekelys of northern Transylvania, was in the living quarters of the coach house. He was sitting at the rough wooden kitchen table, shining a collection of hunting boots. He had plenty of time. The master, Dinu Krymlac, was away on business in Craiova, in southwestern Wallachia, and would not be back for some days. Only his daughter, Maria, and a couple of maids were in the large house to which Veidt's humble but comfortable quarters were attached. It was late and by now, no doubt, Maria and the others would have gone to bed. Veidt smiled to himself. He was the only one around who had not retired. Even his faithful guard dog, Zoltan, seemed asleep. The large, smooth-haired Dobermann pinscher sprawled at his feet, his collar chain snaking a little way across the stone floor to a short wooden post.

Veidt turned back to his boot blacking, spitting copiously on the toecap of a fine pair of riding boots and rubbing in a generous smear of polish, working it in with a rag, around and around, until the cap shone like a coating of ice. At length, he completed the task and placed the boots down neatly, side by side with the other pairs he had already finished cleaning. He was a tall, wiry man whose long, sinuous frame and thinning, wispy brown hair belied his actual strength. Twenty-five years' service in the Krymlac household, with plenty of fresh air and exercise, had kept his lean-muscled body powerful and well toned. Only the weathered lines about his angular, rather skull-like face and the tiny rivulet creases encircling his thin-lipped mouth made him seem older than his forty years. The eyes that peered out from the dark, swarthy complexion of the typical Rumanian peasant were alert, deep, penetrating and fathomless.

Veidt was about to reach into the wooden box beside his chair to pick out yet another pair of boots to buff and polish, when Zoltan began to stir. The dog uttered a low, rumbling growl from deep inside its powerful chest, got to its feet and dashed to the extremity of the chain that tethered it, setting up a loud barking.

"Quiet! Zoltan, quiet!" Veidt hissed, grasping the chain and attempting to pull back the animal. But the dog kept barking. Veidt did not want Zoltan to wake Maria and the two women servants at the rear of the house. He slipped the dog's chain and opened the coach-house door.

"All right, Zoltan!" he said sharply. "Stay out the whole night for all I care!"

The dog bounded immediately out into the yard, still barking, until the sound faded into the distance somewhere in the grounds. Veidt shook his head, closed the door and turned back to his work.

Up in her bedroom at the front of the manor, Maria Krymlac stirred restlessly, but the distant barking of Zoltan had not awakened her fully. She sighed and her breathing soon resumed its steady rhythm once again as she drifted back into deep, restful sleep.

In the corner of the room, something stirred. A swishing sound, like that of long, flowing garments, moved closer to the bed, slowly and stealthily. But the dark, beautiful girl lying there, her hair in raven tresses around her on the pillow, did not stir. A wedge of moonlight angling down through the bedroom window fell suddenly upon the shoulders of the figure that emerged from the corner shadows. The tall silhouette of a man, his broad frame swathed in a long, flowing black cape lined with scarlet satin, was outlined in the silvery half-light. He stood looking down at Maria. Yet his figure cast no shadow upon the bed before him.

Count Igor Dracula drew back the folds of his billowing cape as he moved closer and closer to the sleeping girl. His pallid, flour-colored face was haloed with a handsome head of hair, graying at the temples, swept back aristocratically from the brow and over his ears. His eyes were focused with a magnetic intensity upon Maria. His thin, pale lips slowly parted, revealing his teeth, the two canines at either side unusually long, extending over his lower lip in slightly curved, razor-sharp pointed fangs. He drew a barely audible deep breath, then leaned down over the slumbering girl, his jaw opening as his face inclined toward her bare white neck.

Even though she slept, Maria suddenly instinctively became aware of a presence, of something looming over her. Her eyes darted open and she was confronted with the gloating grimace of the Count, only inches away from her face. The Count himself, momentarily startled by her awakening, froze, absolutely immobile where he stood, his body arched over Maria's bed. Then she screamed, a shrill, piercing shriek of terror that penetrated the silence of the night.

Below in the yard, Zoltan began his loud barking once again, and within moments, footsteps sounded on the wooden floor of the corridor out beyond the bedroom. The Count quickly gathered himself and stood upright. He swept his cape around him and turned to survey the room rapidly. The window was still open, as he had left it upon his entry. With two strides he had reached it and, raising his cape up on either side of him with his hands, stood for a brief second like some gigantic, nightmarish bird. Maria, paralyzed with fear, could scarcely believe her eyes at what happened next. There was a sudden whooshing sound, like the noise of heavy cloth drapes being unfurled, and the silhouette of the great winged figure at the window inexplicably and instantly appeared to shrink. Maria blinked and caught only the vague, flickering impression of something small, animal and leathery, disappearing out of the window with a peculiar, irregular flapping sound, like that of a book being hurled through the air, its pages fluttering open.

Next, Maria heard Veidt's voice ring out, alarmed, from the other side of the bedroom door.

"Maria! Are you all right?"

Prompted by her scream and the resumed barking of his dog, Veidt had dashed immediately upstairs to her room. Within a second, he was in the room, looking rapidly around, then placing his arm around her shoulders comfortingly. Maria, still unable to speak, shuddered and sobbed with uncontrollable shock at what she had experienced.

Below in the yard Zoltan's mighty barks continued to rend the night air, and Veidt thought: Dogs do not bark at nightmares. Then, quite unexpectedly, his guard dog's yelps subsided into a whine, followed by whimpering and then silence. Veidt turned his attention back to the sobbing girl.

Outside Zoltan stood bolt upright, panting slightly but looking straight ahead, almost trancelike. It had been Maria's scream, followed by the sight of a small bat, no bigger than a human hand, fluttering out of her bedroom window that had originally caused the dog to bark. Now, however, he remained perfectly still and silent as the tiny creature lay upon his neck. It hung there, quivering, as it received the blood it was lapping from the dog's throat through the two tiny incisions it had made with its needlelike fangs. Still the great dog stood there, unconcerned, as the loathsome little mammal feasted.

Zoltan did not even look up as an oil lamp was kindled in the bedroom of Maria, casting its flickering light upon the window frame. He remained totally immobile still when the bat gently detached itself from his neck.

Next, Zoltan seemed to be emerging from a remote daze and raised his head to look up at the figure of a man standing over him; a man whom he had not seen before and yet who his instincts told him was vaguely familiar. The man's piercing eyes gazed down into Zoltan's face. The dog heard no audible sound, and yet the man's command was perfectly clear: "Come." And as the man strode off in the light mists along the darkened drive leading away from the Krymlac manor, it seemed only natural to the great dog to follow. . . .

The huge hound stood stock still in the underground crypt, like someone in a daydream. A slight noise, of more crumbling debris, made him start and brought him back to his present senses. He looked around. The uniformed soldier on the floor of the vault did not stir. Zoltan felt strange . . . curiously disoriented. He sensed that he was no longer quite the same, with his huge fanged jaws, his greater strength and his imperfect animal impression of added preternatural intelligence and senses. No . . . not the same dog that had awakened that night long ago and barked, until his master, Veidt Smit, had unchained him and let him out. His master! Now he remembered!

The powerful beast turned around. There, in the wall, next to the yawning hole from which his own casket had tumbled, was another, now also slightly dislodged. Zoltan moved toward it, sniffing. He pawed at the plaque which formed the outer end of the sarcophagus. The inscription read: VEIDT SMIT, 1630–1670.

Zoltan whimpered excitedly as he caught the faintest trace of a familiar scent and began to claw and scratch at the crumbling plasterwork seal around the coffin until, piece by piece, it fell away under the efforts of his hammer paws. Seizing the edge of the sarcophagus in his gaping jaws, the dog began to heave, digging in his feet as his muscular frame tugged backward with savage jerks. Slowly, inch by inch, the coffin slid from its aperture, falling eventually with a resounding crash to the floor of the crypt. Once it lay amid the dusty debris, Zoltan stood over it, panting. After a moment, he took the over-hanging edge of the coffin lid in his teeth and tugged with all his might. The lid creaked . . . and moved a fraction. Zoltan jerked upward, wrenching with all the strength of his brawny neck and shoulders. The lid groaned and gave way. With one last heave, the hound lifted again and, plac-ing his paws on the coffin's edge, pushed and thrust the lid until it fell open sideways, crashing to the vault floor.

Zoltan peered inside. Beneath the musty winding sheet lay the vague form of a man. But at the position where the head should have been, only a hideous skull grinned mockingly out at him. A large wooden stake protruded from the area of the rib cage. The dog moved toward it and grasped it in his jaws, but found it difficult to get a firm grip, leaning as he was over the coffin's edge. With a bound, Zoltan leaped into the coffin astride the bony, shrouded remains and took a fresh hold of the stake, this time in a vise-like grip. The muscles in the brute's neck, thick as the thigh of an athlete, tautened as he strained and heaved upon the wooden shaft. At last, with a powerful wrench, the stake came free and Zoltan leaped from the coffin. He crouched beside the casket, ears pointing forward, eagerly watching, the thick wooden stake still clenched between his jaws, saliva dripping from his bared gums to mingle with the dark-red stain on the pointed rod's end.

Beneath the folds of grave linen, a slight stirring began. Flesh began gradually to form on the grinning skull. Where the rib cage had thrust upward skeletally, there began a spasmodic, irregular movement of labored breathing. Hair began to sprout on the head of the slowly materializing face in the casket. And within a few moments, there before Zoltan, eyes closed, lay the seemingly sleeping form of Veidt Smit—his old master!

The eyes flickered open. The breathing, at first labored and heavy, settled down to a more moderate, natural rhythm. Veidt looked slowly about him, trying to focus. His eyes fell eventually on the giant hound, sitting staring at him, and faint recognition dawned on Veidt's sunken features. And, although he did not speak, Zoltan seemed to hear once more his master's compelling, sepulchral voice:

"Zoltan . . . at last!"

Slowly, carefully, as if unused to the envelope of flesh he had reinhabited only moments before, Veidt reached out, grasping each side of the coffin with his wiry, tapering fingers, and pulled himself gradually up into a sitting position. He carefully turned back the winding sheet in which he had lain and, for a second or two, studied the all-black clothing in which he was dressed. He kicked down the folds of shroud from his legs and feet and rose, stepping gently, silently from the coffin. Zoltan sat motionless, watching. Veidt extended his hand and took the wooden stake from between the dog's jaws. With his other hand, he gently patted the broad, flat head of the unearthly hound. And again, though Veidt communicated in no natural way, Zoltan seemed to hear his old master's eerie voice speak his name: "Zoltan . . ."

Eagerly, Zoltan rose and made once more for the wall of shelved sarcophagi. He stood up on his hind legs, practically dwarfing the straight-backed, lean figure of his master, and began to claw at the upper casket in the first of the vertical rows: the coffin of Count Igor Dracula. Veidt quickly understood and stepped toward his former watchdog to help. Zoltan moved aside slightly as Veidt tried to prise open the casket drawer, but it was well sealed. Suddenly, both man and dog stood stock still, listening. A low rumbling noise issued from somewhere in the bowels of the earth. Cracks slowly appeared in the walls of the sepulcher and rocks began to crumble away from the ceiling. Zoltan eagerly renewed his pounding efforts to reopen Count Igor's sealed resting place, clawing desperately at the stone plaque, his whining growing louder and louder until it was an ear-jarring screech.

The trembling of the earth rumbled ominously closer and Veidt quickly realized their immediate danger of being buried by falling rocks. He grasped the great hound by the neck, pulling him away from his efforts at the wall. Reluctantly and still whining piteously, the dog allowed him to steer him toward the steps, leading out of the crypt. As they reached the foot of the stone stairway, the geological disturbance reached its peak and enormous hunks of rock crashed down from the ceiling of the vault, burying the still-inert body of Private Laszlo Vukanovic. Veidt and Zoltan had barely made it to the summit of the stairs and out into the night before the whole of the vault caved in completely, including the narrow ascending passage they had ascended. Tons of soil and rock tumbled inward and a great dust pall rose, almost as if the very earth itself were protesting, trying to ensure that no further blasphemous, undead abominations should emerge from the vault, the secret resting place of the last of the Draculas.

Several hundred yards away from the cave-in, Veidt considered it safe to pause. He halted and, obediently, Zoltan stopped, squatted beside him and gazed up into his face inquiringly. Once again the animal began to whine pitifully, his powerful voice echoing away through the foothills of the Carpathians. Veidt glanced around anxiously, fearful that the dog's wails might attract the attention of some wayfarer. He grabbed Zoltan by the neck and shoulders and, with a great deal of effort, managed to force him into a lying position. Kneeling beside him, he looked full into the creature's face, his hypnotic, hooded eyes boring deep into those of the dog. His wrinkled, tight-lipped mouth spread sideways in a strange, knowing, eerie smile. And once again, though Veidt did not speak, Zoltan understood.

"I promise you, Zoltan," Veidt's outré, telepathic "voice" seemed to say, "we will find our master."

Protection against vampirism . . . ranged from transfixing the corpse with a stake (made of aspen, maple, blackthorn or hawthorn, depending on local belief) to lopping off the head, and from burning the corpse to ashes to tearing out the heart and throwing boiling water or oil onto the grave. . . .

The aspen tree was said to have furnished wood for the cross whilst the whitethorn was described by Sir John Mandeville . . . "there the Jewes scorned Him and maden Him a crown of branches of the Albiespyne, that is, Whitethorn . . ."

—Anthony Masters, *The Natural History of the Vampire* (Putnam, 1972)

FOUR:

Bring Out Your Undead

Captain Gheorghita's men had been working since first light with pick, ropes and shovel, clearing away the massive chunks of jagged, fractured rock from the collapsed tomb. They had managed to unearth four or five of the wooden coffins from the blocked interior, and these were now lying haphazardly on the sparsely tufted earth outside, among the craggy rocks and rubble. By the time Major Badea Hessle arrived at the captain's field-tent headquarters, the crumpled, seemingly lifeless form of Private Laszlo Vukanovic had also been discovered, lifted from the vault and placed under a blanket some twenty-five yards away.

Captain Gheorghita ordered one of his men to radio for an ambulance, then he and Major Hessle walked up the mountainside toward the excavation. Major Hessle, a stocky, brusque-mannered woman in her thirties, seemed deliberately to have hidden her natural attractiveness under her green army hat, set mannishly at an angle, her lengthy skirt and her pristine white freshly laundered shirt with its military button-down pockets and epaulettes. As she strode along beside him, Captain Gheorghita could not help wondering how she would look with a trace of makeup, a modest décolletage and a pair of more feminine shoes than the standard army brogues she wore.

"Has everyone been accounted for?" she asked, waving an arm vaguely in the direction of the toiling squad of soldiers.

"There was only one guard on duty at the time of the cave-in," the captain said. "He's still alive."

As the pair neared the cluster of coffins, battered and dusty, lying on the ground, they were joined by a man in civilian clothes. He wore a neat gray Homburg which matched his heavy tweed suit, the jacket cut in the Norfolk style, with a half-belt and pleated slashes. He was in his early fifties, and though full graying beard tended to give him a slightly fossilized, professorial look, his face was friendly and his eyes signaled a mind that was sharp, alert and finely honed. Captain Gheorghita turned as the newcomer reached them.

"Major Hessle," he said, "this is Inspector Branco."

"Honored, Inspector," the major said, taking the detective's hand. "I've heard of you."

Branco grinned amusedly.

"Yes . . . I know. I believe we share the same interests."

There was the faint semblance of a quizzical tone in his voice, but Major Hessle did not reply. She was quickly turning over in her mind what she had read of the famous Inspector. Vaclav Branco, detective, formerly of the University of Graz, in Styria; folklorist, author of several books on criminology and the mythology of rural Eastern Europe and an expert in particular, it was said, on vampirism, the cult of the undead.

The trio strolled on until they came to within a few yards of the group of laboring soldiers at the caved-in entrance to the underground vault. Captain Gheorghita extended an arm, indicating that this was as far as it was safe to go without protective helmets.

"Lucky the entire mountain didn't collapse," Major Hessle said, surveying the scene. "We'd never have been able to dig our way inside otherwise."

Inspector Branco nodded, exhaling thoughtfully as he gazed at a stack of coffins recently removed from the working.

"Does the tomb interest you, Major?" he asked at length.

"Yes. And you?"

Branco wondered if the major's interest lay specifically in the same area as his own. She was, he knew, an archaeologist attached to the army. But what, if anything, did she know of vampirism?

"In this part of the country," he said guardedly, "*every* tomb interests me. The history of this region has not always been a happy one, as you well know." He looked at the captain. "The officer here is a little skeptical and impatient."

Major Hessle glanced at the captain inquiringly. He gave her an apologetic grimace.

"I am only here to carry out my orders," Captain Gheorghita said.

"I know you will understand, Captain," Major Hessle said. "The importance of what the Inspector is trying to get across to you is that the underground blasting uncovered a *Dracula* tomb."

Branco sighed relievedly. So she did know something. He would not be entirely alone, surrounded by skeptics. These cases were always so difficult. Captain Gheorghita stood by silently, noncommittal.

"Come," said Major Hessle, taking the inspector's arm. "Let's take a closer look now."

The pair walked off, leaving Captain Gheorghita staring vaguely after them. He stood there for some moments, deep in thought, and was only brought back to the present when the figure of Captain Thurko suddenly appeared at his elbow.

"Who is he?" Captain Thurko asked, nodding at the retreating back of Inspector Branco.

Captain Gheorghita looked at his fellow officer. "Inspector Branco," he said simply, then added with a hesitant note of disbelief: "He's a leading authority on . . . vampirism."

Captain Thurko shrugged, and the two officers wandered up the slope, following Branco and the major. When they reached the group of coffins, Major Hessle was kneeling down beside one of the relics. She looked up at Branco questioningly. He nodded.

"You there!" the major called to three soldiers who stood by, leaning on their shovels, looking on. "Pry these open."

The soldiers glanced briefly at each other, hesitantly. They had seen the body of their comrade, Private Vukanovic, being hauled from the vault, and, what with the number of ancient caskets, a certain uneasiness had prevailed among all the men since the clearing operation began. Major Hessle flashed them an admonitory look. Reluctantly, the soldiers put down their shovels, took up chisels and crowbars and set to, prising open the first of the six coffins lying around.

The wooden lid groaned as the last of its corroded screws gave way, and the coffin lay open. In it was a white-shrouded body with a wooden stake protruding from the position of its chest. Inspector Branco looked knowingly at the major and nodded with a sigh of resignation. He had been correct all along; a vampire tomb had been accidentally unearthed.

It took Major Hessle some moments to recover her voice, after gazing at the grisly remains in the casket, a long-dead member of the legendary Dracula clan, a bloodied patch staining its covering sheet where the wooden stake had done its unsavory, but necessary, work. She signaled the soldiers to replace the coffin lid, then, when they had done so, ordered: "Open each one of these."

One by one, the caskets were forced open, each time to reveal a shrouded, crumpled form, every one pinioned by a wooden stake. The freshness of the gentle mountain air currents was quickly overtaken by the stench of death and advanced decomposition, wafted to the nostrils of the onlookers.

Major Hessle rose to her feet as the men continued to open and reseal each coffin in turn under the stern watchfulness of Inspector Branco.

"Excuse us for a moment," she said to the two officers and men, and drew the inspector away from the coffins and the excavated tomb. Below, at the foot of the mountainside, a sudden flurry of movement caught the inspector's eye. A straggled line of soldiers was holding back a group of civilians, curious peasants who were trying to get up the mountain to see what was going on.

"You were right," Major Hessle said resignedly, not noticing what was happening below. "Definitely a vampire tomb."

Branco pointed to the little mob at the foot of the slopes.

"I know these villagers," he said. "If word gets out about this, the whole countryside will be terrorized."

"No question about that," the major agreed.

"Then . . . you know what we must do?" Branco said, gravely stroking his beard. Major Hessle looked at him and slowly nodded.

She turned back to face the soldiers, who had now finished their work on the coffins. "Lieutenant!" she called. A young officer stepped forward the few paces toward them. He saluted.

"Burn every one of these coffins!" Major Hessle ordered.

"But, Major—"

"Every single one of them—that's an order!" she said firmly.

40

"Yes, Major." The lieutenant saluted again, wheeled and marched back up the slope.

"That should do it, Inspector," the major said.

Branco nodded thoughtfully.

Beyond them, near the mouth of the vault, four soldiers had carried out the remaining two coffins from among the rubble and placed them on the ground. Branco watched as they were set down, then a private looked up toward himself and the major.

"Major Hessle!"

Other soldiers clustered around the two latest coffins, staring down puzzledly as Major Hessle and Inspector Branco made their way toward them. Branco pushed his way through the small knot of men, clearing a way through for the major. The pair gazed down into the coffins momentarily, then looked, baffled, at each other. Both caskets were empty.

"How do you account for this, Inspector?" Major Hessle said at last.

He drew her away from the others, then sighed, shaking his head.

"I can't," he said simply.

Captain Gheorghita appeared beside them. His uniform was coated with a fine layer of dust.

"There are no more bodies inside that tomb, Major," he said. "We've been at it all day. The only other one we found was that guard over there. Otherwise, the vault is completely cleared."

He pointed as he spoke toward the place where a field ambulance had now pulled up beside the form of Private Vukanovic, lying on the ground, covered up to his neck by a blanket. Two ambulance men were crouching over him.

The inspector shot Major Hessle a dark, wary glance and she moved off, heading for the place where the inert soldier lay. Branco and Captain Gheorghita followed at her heels. As they moved off, a group of soldiers were making their way up the slope carrying five-gallon drums of kerosene, ready to begin the mass cremation of the coffins and their occupants.

"Is this man alive?" Major Hessle asked the ambulance men impatiently. The uniformed attendants stood up.

"His pulse is beating faintly, Major," one of them said. "But we find no sign of breathing."

Inspector Branco stepped quickly forward in front of the major and knelt beside the prostrate soldier. He pulled back the blanket slightly, then gently turned the soldier's head from side to side. On the left side of Vukanovic's neck were two round punctures, ringed with clotted blood. Branco stood up and looked sharply at Major Hessle. Indicating the ambulance attendants with a slight nod of his head, he said sternly:

"Tell them to return to the hospital and leave the guard with us."

Major Hessle looked at the first ambulance man and nodded her assent. The man looked shocked.

"I take full responsibility," Major Hessle said. "Do as I say."

The ambulance men moved off, climbed into their vehicle and began to back down the uneven slopes. At the foot the group of villagers were still being held back by a line of soldiers.

Captain Gheorghita was staring incredulously at Branco, but the latter did not meet his gaze. The captain was about to say something, but changed his mind when he saw the detective bend down to pick up a splintered shard of wood which had broken from the lid of one of the opened coffins. Captain Gheorghita noticed that a light film of perspiration had broken out on Branco's brow as he took out a clasp knife and, grim-faced, began to whittle the end of the wooden stave into a sharp point.

Species: Varcolaco—Murohy—Strigoi
Characteristics: Can take on the characteristics of a dog, a cat, a frog, a toad, a
louse, a flea, a spider . . .

—Ornella Volta, *The Vampire*
(Tandem Books, 1965)

FIVE:

Branco—Vampire Hunter

For the second time in two days an enormous blanket of billowing black smoke
loomed over the Carpathian mountainside.
But on this occasion it came not from an
explosion, but from a massive pyre of wood
doused in kerosene. Atop the blazing wood,
whose heat drove back the soldiers who had
kindled it, lay heaped the twelve coffins
found in the subterranean vault.

As dusk approached, Inspector Branco
glanced down the valley and was relieved
to see that the curious villagers who had
congregated there earlier had gone. He had
asked Captain Gheorghita to speak to them

and try to persuade them that there was no point in hanging around.

At Branco's feet lay the body of Private Laszlo Vukanovic. His eyes were closed, the face muscles were relaxed, and the skin had taken on the waxen pallor of death. The inspector's improvised wooden stake, now protruding from the soldier's chest, had done its work. Neither he nor the burning corpses on the giant pyre nearby would ever again be among the legions of the undead, vampires who preyed upon the living, gradually draining their blood until they too became vampiric, lying dormant in their coffins by day, seeking out victims for their unholy feasts by night, between the hours of sunset and cockcrow.

Major Hessle and Captain Gheorghita stood by as Branco slowly drew the thick gray blanket over the face of the dead soldier. Turning to the captain, Major Hessle said: "Burn him with the rest of them." She spoke matter-of-factly, not allowing any emotion to color her voice. The captain raised a protesting eyebrow.

"Major . . . are you aware that this man is a soldier!" he said with indignation.

"*Was* a soldier, Captain," Major Hessle corrected him.

"Yes," Inspector Branco put in. "A soldier of Dracula. Burn him!"

Still unable to comprehend fully the need to burn the corpse, not realizing that someone had only to remove the stake to cause Private Vukanovic to revive again as a vampire, Captain Gheorghita met Branco's stern gaze. He saw the imperative look in the detective's eyes and, resignedly, turned and nodded to two of his men standing by. The soldiers picked up the gray limp bundle and moved off toward the macabre bonfire.

Branco stared into the flames, deep in thought. Something was still troubling him. It was not the final, horrifying gasp of agony that the young soldier had emitted as Branco had performed his unsavory task and driven home the wooden stake. Nor was it the momentary look of utter loathing and hatred upon the poor creature's face before he slumped back in death. No . . . there was something else; something much more urgent to be cleared up. Who had occupied those two empty coffins? And where were the occupants now?

Major Hessle had needed no persuading when Inspector Branco invited her back to his headquarters in Bucharest. Simply to work with this famous detective on what was possibly the most unusual and fascinatingly sinister of cases in her career was a great honor in itself, one that she could barely refuse.

But by dawn the following day, she was beginning to envy the inspector his untiring thoroughness, his seemingly inexhaustible energy. Throughout the night they had sat in Branco's private library at police headquarters, drinking numerous cups of coffee and poring over documents from dusty spring-clip box files and heavy tomes which, from time to time, the inspector had hefted from the shelves that covered every wall of his study. The desk before them was piled high with ancient books, folders and files, genealogies and case histories, newspaper clippings and confidential police records.

Laboriously, the inspector had traced the lineage of practically every known vampire-tainted family over a vast area of Eastern Europe: the Yorgas of Styria, the Bathorys of Wallachia, the bloodthirsty boyar warlords of medieval Transylvania, including, of course, the infamous Draculas.

As he proceeded, the inspector had explained the various types and strains of vampires, demonstrating his amazing, encyclopedic knowledge of the subject: the *mjertovjec* species of Russia, the *Nachzehrer* of Bavaria, the *ogeljen* of Bohemia, the *Krvopijac* of Bulgaria, and the *varcolaco, murohy* and *strigoi* of Rumania. Each had its own characteristics, activities and distinguishing features. Each its own peculiarities and *modus operandi.* There were quite specific methods of disposal for each individual species, too: by the stake, by fire, by beheading, by exorcism, by natural running water, and so on. Some types were active only at particular times of the year or phases of the

47

moon, others were restricted by the availability of the victims upon which they depended, whether child, adult or animal.

Major Hessle read learned articles by anthropologists, psychologists and biologists from practically every part of the globe; treatises that attempted to explain the origins and causes of vampirism, theses on the possibilities of shape-shifting, reports of psychiatrists on cannibalistic traits in human beings and theories claiming that most alleged vampire phenomena were the result of premature burials in less enlightened times.

Inspector Branco, meanwhile, pored over his volumes and papers, pausing occasionally to explain a point or to read out accounts of surprisingly recent vampire activity in France, Germany, Spain, Italy and Eastern Europe.

Once or twice during her all-night delving into realms of the utterly fantastic, Major Hessle felt herself giving in to the encroaching fatigue that constantly dogged her. Without realizing it, she would close her eyes briefly to rest them, then jerk awake suddenly to look around, wondering where she was and how long she had been asleep. Inspector Branco either did not notice or failed to acknowledge that he was aware of these lapses on her part. He continued to open and close various heavy volumes, frequently rising to reach for yet further sources of information in his tireless search for clues.

Below in the city streets, traffic noises eventually began to drift into Major Hessle's consciousness and she became aware that a dull gray light, announcing the approach of dawn, was filtering into the sky beyond the buildings opposite police headquarters. At length, Branco looked up and smiled wearily.

"I think I have it," he said.

"I have narrowed it down to only one. I have accounted for all the others we burned."

Major Hessle hurriedly collected her thoughts.

"But there were *two* empty coffins," she protested.

Branco sighed frustratedly.

"I'm sure there's an answer to this, but I can't find it," he said. "All I can account for is one."

His finger on the page of an open book before him, he took up a pen and scribbled on a notepad at his elbow. Then he looked up at her.

"A 'fractional lamia'—that's what it was," he said.

"Fractional lamia?" the major said, puzzled. "What does that mean?"

"It means someone only part vampire," Branco answered. "A real asset to a Dracula."

"In what way?"

"In many ways," Branco explained. "Unlike their masters, they can function in the daytime. They can be trusted to find victims. And most important, they have no craving for blood. That is what Veidt Smit was—Igor Dracula's perfect servant."

Lamia, Branco went on to explain, was originally a Greek and Roman name used to describe a vampire creature in ancient times. It had, however, since come to be used to denote a peculiar variational condition of vampirism. Through some as yet undetermined factor—possibly a subtle genetic flaw in the physical makeup of the victim—the fractional lamia inherited neither his attacker's bloodlust nor his need to lie within the protection of his coffin during daylight hours. Whereas sunlight would sear and blast the body of a true vampire, reducing the creature to dust, it had no such effect on the lamia strain. The lamia was, however, in the state known as undead because it had, in fact, died and risen again after being preyed upon by a vampire. It could be destroyed in the manner most commonly employed for disposing of vampires—impaling with a stake of whitehorn, aspen, maple, blackthorn or hawthorn, beheading or cremation.

The few case histories which had been collected dealing with fractional lamias of this type, Branco explained, had generally not been of aristocratic stock. They were usually of a peculiarly subservient nature, almost in the same way that certain psychological types had an inbred need to be dominated.

The major was silent for some moments, trying to take in what Branco had told her and apply it to the case in question.

"Then actually," she said at length, "he is better off. He has no cravings, and therefore does not live in danger."

"Wrong!" Branco said, closing the book emphatically. "They can't exist without a master. And if my thinking is correct, Major, Veidt Smit right now is searching for his."

Major Hessle looked perplexed.

"But . . . where would he find him?" she said hesitantly. "There are no Draculas left."

"No *vampire* Draculas left, Major," the inspector corrected her. "In my research, I found that thirty years ago, a young Michael Dracula, the last of the Dracula line, left the country for his own safety."

"And where is he now?"

Branco reached into a desk drawer and extracted a small black notebook.

"In America," he said. He flipped through the pages. "Let's see . . . here it is: 14581 Kittridge Street, Tarzana, Los Angeles, California. That's as of two years ago."

Major Hessle leaned forward.

"You think he's still alive?"

"I'm sure," Branco said. "And if he is, Veidt Smit will find him."

The major frowned.

"Smit must be stopped then. At all costs!"

The inspector leaned back in his chair, stretched his arms and legs, then got up. He put away the notebook, took out a handkerchief and drew it across his brow. He leaned forward, placing both hands on his desk, and looked at her squarely. His eyes took on their usual alertness. He no longer seemed even slightly weary in the patch of light beaming in through the library window.

"Major," he said, "I should like that assignment."

Without hesitation, Major Hessle nodded.

"I'll arrange for a special visa for you, Inspector," she said. "It might take a few days, but I'll try to get priority."

Branco nodded his thanks and smiled warmly.

"It is most important that you keep in touch with me," Major Hessle said as Branco helped her into her topcoat.

"Of course," he said.

"You never know when I will have something on that *missing* vampire, Inspector."

They went out and down the corridor.

"I wonder who was in that other coffin . . ." Major Hessle said.

As they left the corridor and turned into the stairway, the major and her bearded companion failed to notice a faint movement in a shadowy alcove. There, standing silently, a look of triumph on his dark-eyed, cadaverous face, stood Veidt Smit. He glanced down at the scrap of paper upon which he had scribbled something. It was headed: Michael Drake, nee Dracula. Beneath was written the

Los Angeles address which the inspector had unwittingly read out a few moments earlier. A thin smile creased the pale, narrow lips of Veidt Smit, the fractional lamia.

. . . lamias haunt cemeteries, disinter corpses . . .

—Collin de Plancy, *Dictionnaire Infernal* (1863)

SIX:

Strange Cargo

The Atlantic crossing had been calm and clear, but as the small freighter rounded the southern tip of Lower California, heavy mists rolled seaward from the cooling landmass of Mexico. Veidt Smit stood at the rail, listening to the low, plaintive call of the ship's foghorn and its lonely echo off the rocks of Ballenas Bay, deadened by the swirling mists.

There were only a handful of passengers traveling steerage on the vessel, and Veidt was content to be alone in the warm, damp night, with the pale light of the full moon barely filtering through the gloom. He wandered down the deck, trailing his hand along the rail, then paused to lean on it. As he stood, the voices of a young couple drifted to his ears from farther forward, but he barely paid any attention to their conversation.

The couple had been taking a stroll around the deck before turning in. The freighter was due to put in at the Port of Los Angeles at San Pedro shortly before daybreak and would disembark at first light.

"I hate to think how long this trip was before they built the Panama," the young man said, stifling a yawn.

"I wish it were longer—I loved every minute of it," came the soft voice of his companion.

"All good things come to an end, honey," the man said. "We'd better get some sleep—we dock in the morning."

The couple's footsteps sounded on the deck and they approached and passed without even noticing the presence of the black-clad figure staring thoughtlessly out into the nothingness of the swirling mists. The pale, opaque vapors, wreathing gently against the hull, wafted by the light Pacific inshore breezes, eventually lulled Veidt into a mood of vague recollections; memories of a similar dark and misty moonlit night long, long ago. More than three centuries ago, to be precise. And even after such a yawning lapse of time, spent lying in the black limbo of a sealed tomb, Veidt was still able to recall in some mystic, unearthly way the events leading up to his eternal allegiance to his adopted master, Count Igor Dracula. . . .

He was rounding the outside of the Krymlac manor house, having dashed down the shadowy oak-paneled staircase and out through a side door. There, striding off across the grounds, was a tall, black-caped figure and, at his heels, Veidt's dog, Zoltan, trotting along obediently. Angrily, Veidt ran after the strange interloper, calling his dog's name. Could this man, he wondered as he ran, have somehow been the cause of Maria's distress, gaining entry to her chamber in the dead of night? There must be some connection between the sudden disturbed barking of Zoltan earlier, then the girl's terrified scream and subsequent hysteria.

Without warning, the tall figure halted and wheeled, his cape whirling around him with a majestic air of command. The stranger gazed directly, arrogantly, into Veidt's eyes. Veidt halted abruptly in his tracks, his mouth open with surprise at the sight of the unfamiliar, yet imposing and aristocratic figure before him. At last, he managed to ask somewhat haltingly:

"Who are you? Where are you taking my dog?"

Veidt tried to look down at the great gray-black hound now seated patiently at the stranger's feet. But the eyes of the man burned into his own with a fierce, compelling intensity and it was a few seconds before Veidt was able to make an active effort to break the man's hypnotic gaze. At last he was somehow able to cast a glance at the dog. It had changed in an uncanny, unnerving manner. Zoltan, once the faithful, warm-eyed, tail-wagging guard dog of the stablemaster, was now a fierce, terrifying, alien beast without a spark of friendliness in its features. Its coat had turned to a dark, velveteen sheen, giving the animal an almost ephemeral quality. Its eyes glowed green and evil with utter hatred, while giant fangs protruded from its snout, lips pulled back over the elongated canines in a permanent snarl of utter loathing and bestiality. The mouth was stained with gouts of blood that shined darkly. Somehow, Zoltan had been instantly and utterly transformed into a hellish brute; a creature not of this world, but of the dark abyss of man's most hideous nightmares.

As he stared unbelievingly, Veidt heard for the first time the deep, sepulchral voice of the man confronting him.

"Come, Veidt Smit," the man said. "I will not deprive you of your dog."

Dimly, Veidt next recalled the stranger reaching forward, enveloping him in his satin-lined cape. He remembered the icy clutch of the stranger's hand and the fetid stench of his breath as the man leaned toward his throat. Then . . . nothing.

All he ever knew from that moment was that he was no longer in the service of the Krymlacs, but a slave to the Draculas; that it was his unavoidable duty only to serve them unfailingly . . . and for eternity.

Veidt took a deep breath and his reverie faded to an abrupt realization that he was no longer in Transylvania, but leaning on a ship's rail, off the southern reaches of the California coastline; that it was not 1670 any more; but 1977. And he had a mission to perform. He moved off along the deck to the hatchway leading down into the freight storage hold, in the belly of the ship. Silently, Veidt walked among the stacked crates and trunks that had turned the hold into a minia-ture labyrinth. Before a medium-sized crate, shaped vaguely like a stunted coffin, he stopped and put a hand on the lid.

There was a low, animal murmur and a faint stirring from within the sealed packing crate. With one hand still on the lid, Veidt bent low with his face close to the side of the box. His dark, fathomless eyes glowed with an eager intensity and his lips writhed into a tight parody of a smile, as he whispered in his emotionless, aspirant way:

"Soon, Zoltan . . . soon."

Early the next morning, the long straight span of a steel bridge came into view forward and beyond it, the hulking, cereal-box cluster of the city of Los Angeles, haloed in a light haze of yellow smog. Before it reached the bridge, the freighter turned to port and hove to at one of the quaysides of San Pedro. As the crates and boxes were hauled by crane from below and deposited on the pier, Veidt stood alone at the rail above the bridge, watching silently. When he recognized the crate bearing Zoltan he waited patiently until it had been lifted ashore, then walked down the gangplank to stand beside it. Two uniformed customs officials were gradually picking their way along the dock, making notes as they checked over the various items of cargo. A member of the ship's crew, carrying a clip-board inventory and a wad of bills of lading, accompanied them, from time to time checking his papers as the customs men asked questions about various items.

At length, they reached the crate beside which the figure of Veidt stood, silent and motionless in dark-tinted shades and black topcoat.

"What do we have here?" one of the customs men inquired, pointing to the crate with his pen. The crewman checked his inventory.

"Hunting dog," he said. "Its owner wanted him shipped back for burial. The papers are all in order—here."

The customs man ignored the proferred documents.

"Open it," he said.

Obligingly, Veidt lifted the lid of the crate after the second customs officer had prised it open on one side. A plain wooden coffin lay within. Veidt reached down and lifted off the lid of this, too.

The customs men and the crewman gaped

down open-mouthed at the enormous gray-black dog, apparently dead, lying on its side on folds of soft black velvet within the coffin. Veidt stood by, expressionless behind his dark glasses. One of the customs men bent down and swiftly felt around the inert form of the dog, lifting its huge head to examine the coffin lining beneath. When he had finished, the dog's head flopped lifelessly back to its velvet pillow. The man then checked around the rest of the interior and stood up.

"Sorry," he said apologetically to Veidt. "Close it up."

As the customs men moved on, the crew member paused to explain to Veidt that there were plenty of services in the San Pedro complex where he could arrange transport to shift the heavy crate. Veidt assured the man that someone would be picking up the crate, but not until after nightfall. That was okay, the man said, he could leave the crate there on the pier as long as he liked. "Let's face it, mister," he grinned sarcastically, "nobody's likely to want to steal that thing." The man went off, laughing to himself, to rejoin the customs checkers.

Veidt made sure the crate was safely re-fastened and himself headed off in the opposite direction, where the man had indicated the passenger facilities were.

It was dark before he returned. The steve-dores and customs men had left the small pier deserted, except for the single wooden crate. Only a few lights burned on the walls of the low, locked-up warehouse buildings. The freighter had sailed again and Veidt thought he could see its tiny lamps disappearing, out beyond the harbor. There was no mist, but once again a pale, watery moon hung in a bed of silver-gray clouds. Veidt looked carefully up and down the dock to make sure no one was around, then stooped to reopen the large wooden crate. Next, he opened the lid of the coffin within.

Zoltan lay unmovingly upon his cushion of velvet folds. The freighter's whistle sounded in the distance as it continued to recede from sight. The dog within the coffin began to stir. In a moment, it sat up, looked around, then clambered out to sit obediently at the feet of its master, craning back its neck to stare up at him questioningly. At a nod from Veidt the pair set off at a brisk walking pace, the bulky shadow of the dog loping along at his master's side.

While Zoltan had lain in his dark resting place on the dockside, Veidt had been out in the suburbs reconnoitering and had found exactly what he wanted. For several miles the pair walked along, through quiet residential areas, the lights from televisions and reading lamps shining warmly in living-room windows, cars parked in driveways and under carports. There was little traffic and no pedestrians to pay any attention to the man in black, apparently walking his dog.

At length, they reached Veidt's goal. The wrought-iron gates to the small out-district cemetery were unlocked and Veidt gently pushed both open, leaving them wide. Leaving the main driveway, Veidt and Zoltan strode off between the well-tended and landscaped graves and tombstones, heading for a low, long building draped in shadow, at the heart of the graveyard. The cemetery caretaker's lodge was a single-story gray brick building, surrounded by a circular drive. Beyond it stood a jet-black station-wagon hearse. There would be no problem. The keys were still in the dashboard, and even if the caretaker did happen to hear the faint purr of the engine, Zoltan would deal with him swiftly.

All that remained now was for Veidt to drive back to the harbor to pick up Zoltan's coffin, in which the dog would rest during daylight hours. Then their search for their new master could begin in earnest.

Whilst we were talking we heard a sort of
sound between a yelp and a bark. It was
far away; but the horses got very restless,
and it took Johann all his time to quiet
them. He was pale, and said, "It sounds
like a wolf—but yet there are no wolves
here now."

—Bram Stoker, *Dracula's Guest*
(1914)

SEVEN:

14581 Kittridge Street

There was an air of suppressed excitement
in the Drake household. The television in
the cozy, comfortably furnished den was
switched on, but the sound was turned down
low and none of the four members of the
family was actively paying it any attention.

Michael Drake was sitting on the edge of a
chunky armchair with a folding roadmap
spread across his knees, studying it carefully,
tracing along its markings with a retracted
ballpoint pen. New highways and link roads,
cloverleaf junctions and freeway intersections
had sprouted everywhere since Michael had
last made the journey he was plotting, and he

wanted to be sure not to miss any new time-saving routes.

Across the room in another matching armchair, his wife, Marla, had finished brushing her nape-length, silky auburn hair, and, dressed in relaxing, loose-fitting top and white slacks, she was turning her attention to her traveling manicure kit, making sure all the items were in place: nail file, cuticle remover, scissors, combs, nail-polish remover, clippers and emery boards.

A number of suitcases stood stacked beside the four-seater studio couch while another, not quite fully packed, lay open on the coffee table.

With a gesture of finality, sure now that he had the route firmly in his mind, Michael tapped his map with his pen, then looked up at the two children, clad in matching yellow pajamas, loafing on the thick rug, playing idly with their sprawling sleepy German shepherd, Samson.

"I know it's still early," Michael said. "But we all have to get up at five and I don't want any arguments. Off to bed now."

Ignoring him, Linda, at eight the younger by a year of the two children, chucked Samson playfully under the chin and said, "Mom . . . when can Annie come back inside the house?"

Marla looked up from her manicure kit, got up and switched off the color set.

"Not until we've found homes for her

pups," she said emphatically, as if she were tired of answering the same question over and over.

Michael reached forward and ruffled his daughter's hair, a lighter and longer version of his wife's tresses.

"Don't worry, honey," he said. "Annie's doing just fine in the garage."

He got up and gently took hold of Samson's collar, easing the dog to its feet. Thrusting a forefinger at the dog's upturned, inquiring nose, he added, semi-mockingly: "And you, proud father, belong with your family. Come on. Out!"

The dog allowed Michael to hustle it over to the interconnecting door to the garage, Michael opened it and motioned Samson out. He closed the door once the dog had loped outside, then turned back to his family and announced:

"All right, Marla, kids—let's get some sleep. We'll finish packing in the morning."

Linda was first to jump up with outstretched arms to kiss her father good night, reluctantly followed by her brother, Steve, who had only recently passed his ninth birthday.

A mini-chorus of "good night, Dad," a bustle of slippered feet, and the kids allowed themselves to be ushered upstairs to their rooms by their mother.

Outside in the garage, another young family was settling down for the night. In a

blanket-lined box, two young German shepherd pups were already curled in slumber
while beside the box lay Annie, nose on paws.
Samson sniffed around the edge of Annie's
mat for a moment, peering casually in at the
pups, then lay down beside the mother of
his litter.

Kittridge Street lay deserted, curving lazily
around in a wide arc, its generous lawns
planted with palms and its wide driveways
bathed in soft silver moonlight.

Marla Drake was sitting up in bed, a book
open on her lap, but she was not reading it
as her husband came out of the bathroom in
blue pajamas and darker-blue terrycloth robe.
He went over to a closet and began rummag-
ing about in the top shelf, then closed it and
walked over to a chest of drawers. Working
from the bottom upward, he began to feel
around in each of the drawers.

"What are you looking for?" Marla asked.

"I found it," Michael said, turning as he
closed the top drawer. In his hand was a
revolver. He checked the safety catch, then
looked to see if the chamber was empty.

"Oh, that thing," Marla said.

"Yeah, that thing. Now where'd I put the
bullets?"

"You didn't put the bullets," Marla said.
"I put the bullets—and they're in the garage
in that old trunk of yours."

"Good," Michael said. "I'll get them in the
morning." He wrapped the revolver in a cloth

and slid it into an open zipper bag on a chair beside the chest of drawers. Behind him, Marla sighed somewhat impatiently, closed her book and placed it on the bedside stand. As he turned, Michael could not help noticing the disapproving look on her face.

"Look, I know how you feel about guns," he said. "But on a camping trip, it's necessary."

Marla relaxed her expression into a smile and patted the bed beside her.

"Come and sit here a minute," she said. Michael complied and she took both his hands. "What are we going to do about Steve and Linda?"

"What do you mean?"

Marla shrugged. "They feel bad, leaving the dogs behind," she said.

"We're not leaving them alone," Michael protested. "The Parkses will take good care of 'em."

"Well . . . there's that, too," Marla said. "We're *always* imposing on the Parkses."

Michael spread his hands.

"Marla, what do you want me to do—bring all the dogs?"

"It *would* be a happier trip," Marla said, her head on one side, coyly. Michael closed his eyes, thinking.

"Mmm . . . let's see . . ." he said. "It's only half a day's drive there and back. Once we're settled we can probably fix up something under the camper." He hesitated, then shrugged. "Yeah, okay, it'll work all right."

At his assent, Marla reached forward, her arm's around his neck, pulled him forward and kissed him gently on the mouth.

"That," he said, pulling her closer, "was not a kiss. That was a bribe." And Marla kissed him passionately and lingeringly, pulling him down into the bed.

Down in the garage, Annie and her pups were sound asleep, but Samson suddenly blinked open his eyes and raised his head, his ears upright, alert. He listened attentively, sniffing the air with his head turning around, then slumped back onto his forepaws again.

Outside, two dark shapes had rounded the gentle bend that curved around the front of the Drake household. Veidt and Zoltan approached silently. Before the mailbox numbered 14581 they halted, and the sturdy dog followed the direction of Veidt's gaze to the upper story of the house. The dog went forward up the drive and, almost effortlessly, made one incredible bound, to land on a ledge beside the second-story bedroom windows. Veidt stood below, watching silently.

The dog edged along the ledge until it could peer into the first of the darkened windows. Its eyes narrowed evilly and its huge fangs were bared as it caught sight of a child sleeping within. Then, in the strange, telepathic way that Veidt had, Zoltan heard the voice of his master directing him: "Zoltan, no. The other bedroom."

Precariously balanced, Zoltan turned around, placing his huge paws carefully on the narrow ledge, and crept up to the larger window of the master bedroom. Inside, Michael Drake and his wife now lay asleep.

Suddenly one of Zoltan's paws seemed to slip from under him and a dislodged tile from the roof fell, to shatter on the paved driveway below with a loud report that echoed in the street. Immediately from the garage below, Samson and Annie began barking loudly.

Michael Drake sat up in bed with a start, reached out and punched the switch of the bedside lamp. Marla was also sitting up, looking equally startled. Michael slipped quickly out of bed and headed out into the stair hallway. First, he checked Linda's bedroom, flicking the light on and off briefly, relieved to find that she was still sleeping. Steve stirred only slightly as Michael repeated the procedure in his bedroom, then quietly closed the door.

Outside on the ledge, having backed away from the lighted bedroom window, Zoltan was temporarily distracted by the barking dogs below and looked down at his master, as if waiting for further instructions.

Meanwhile, Michael Drake had dashed downstairs to the hallway, opened the front door of the house and dashed into the garage through a side entrance, without noticing the huge black shape looming overhead on the roof ledge, nor the shadowy figure of a man in black standing motionless by some shrubbery at the end of the driveway.

At a nod from Veidt, Zoltan leaped down from the roof and ran toward his master. Veidt was looking at the garage door through which Drake had entered, but he had closed it behind him.

Inside, the two German shepherds continued to bark furiously.

"Are you crazy?" Michael was shouting, trying to make himself heard above the din. "You be quiet now before you wake up the whole neighborhood! I mean *quiet*—now!"

Somewhat cowed, the two dogs fell to a discontented whining, flopping down in a lying position once more, then fell silent. Michael looked down at them and wagged a threatening finger.

"You want to blow your vacation before you even get started?" he said, quietly now. "Go to sleep."

Annie slumped her head back onto her forepaws again, but Samson continued to sit with his head raised, cocking his ears from side to side, as if he were listening to something out of human hearing, restlessly. Michael went back into the house through the den and, after peering cautiously out both front and rear downstairs windows, to assure himself that there were no prowlers, went back up to bed.

Veidt and Zontan were already on their way back to the stolen station-wagon hearse. The barking of the dogs had caused one or two lights in other houses along Kittridge Street to flick on and Veidt had decided to postpone the attack on his intended victim and master-to-be ... for the time being. The Drake household and Kittridge Street were left once more to the silence of night.

The Wallachians say that a *murony*—a sort of a cross between a werewolf and a vampire connected by name with our nightmare—can take the form of a dog, a cat, or a toad, and also of any bloodsucking insect.

> —W. R. S. Ralston, *Russian Folk Tales* (1873)

EIGHT:

A Hearse on Holiday

Samson's head swiveled back and forth like a spectator watching a tennis match, or one of those infuriatingly fascinating model dogs with wagging articulated heads which drivers often seem to place in their rear windows with the sole object of distracting fellow motorists. He was squatting on the lawn watching as the Drake children and their parents scuttled back and forth, from house to camper and back again, loading up their belongings and necessities. The sleek, long, low camper, the latest thing in mobile luxury, shone dazzling white in the early-morning California sun that bathed the driveway outside 14581 Kittridge Street.

It was still early and none of the neighbors was stirring. Excitedly, Steve and Linda carried the smaller packages and bags of provisions from the kitchen to place them in the holiday vehicle, quickly running back indoors for more. They squabbled briefly as to who should lift in the box containing their two puppies, then compromised and carried it in together. Their father, Michael, hefted the full-size valises of clothing, the packs of sporting equipment and fishing gear, while Marla constantly went around with a concise checklist, making sure that everything that should have been in the camper was no longer in the house, ticking off items as they were removed from the kitchen table and the den armchairs and floor. And all the while, the large German shepherd, Samson, sat like an overseer, scrutinizing every movement carefully.

At last it was time to go around securing the windows, locking the house doors and getting everyone aboard. As Michael bustled the two children toward the camper's open side door, he patted Linda's shoulder.

"You barely touched your breakfast," he said.

"I'm all right, Daddy," Linda beamed, bubbling with eagerness to get going. "I wasn't hungry."

"We'll eat when we get there!" Steve announced, his mood matching that of his sister.

With one foot on the step into the camper, Linda turned impulsively and looked at her father.

"Thank you, Daddy," she said with girlish embarrassment.

"For what?" Michael raised an eyebrow.

"For letting Samson and Annie come along," Steve piped in. At the mention of his name, Samson cocked his ears forward quizzically, but did not move.

"We'll make sure they stay out of your way," Linda assured her father.

Michael grinned wryly, then pantomimed a scowl. "They'd better!" he said. "You kids get inside and watch over your pups."

Steve and Linda clambered aboard and, almost falling over each other, fought playfully for the side seat nearest the corner where the pups lay in their box. Annie was sitting nearby on the floor and Linda began to stroke her fondly.

Michael wandered off to lock the garage, then remembered something and went inside. In a corner stood an old sea-going trunk. He unlocked it and began to rummage among its contents. There was winter clothing in storage, some ski gloves and boots, a clutch of neatly folded college scarves from his own and Marla's alma maters, and a handful of faded old photographs. Among the scarves, Michael felt something solid and pulled out a box of .45-caliber bullets. He checked the contents, slid the box into the pocket of his pale-blue slacks and was about to reclose the trunk when his eye caught the photographs. Casually, he riffled through them. There was one of his mother, taken in the old-fashioned sepia cameo style; a matronly woman in starched white lace and severely scraped-back hair, with the gentle, deeply set eyes of the Slavonic former aristocracy. Then his father, stern and military-looking, in uniform and wearing a long, drooping mustache. They were windows on another world, life-times away, these frozen moments of the past. Next was an ancient, extremely early portrait of a man Michael did not recognize, but who he felt was somehow vaguely familiar: a daguerreotype of a brooding individual in evening dress and opera cape. Then it dawned on Michael—the man bore a vague resemblance to himself: dark, with a slightly olive complexion, firm-lined bone structure and a sturdily set jawline. Possibly an uncle from some distant branch of the family back in the Old Country, Michael thought. Beside the man sat a huge, malevolent-eyed hunting dog of some sort. Michael studied the picture briefly, then skimmed the photographs idly back into the trunk and closed it. He stood, thoughtfully, as if trying to grasp some fleeting, fragmentary memory of something only half-formed, half-shrouded in the mists of subconscious memory. Then Marla's voice from outside broke his incomplete reverie.

"Michael! We're ready!"

Outside, he locked the garage door and turned to see that their neighbor, Pat Parks, was there, talking to Marla. She was in a thick bathrobe and fur slippers, as if she had stepped straight from her bed, or rather, boudoir. She looked extremely attractive even at this hour of the morning, her dark, wine-colored hair framing her high-cheekboned face in sweeping layers and the housecoat, despite its fluffy lining, hugging the contours of her elegantly proportioned figure.

"Morning, Pat," Michael said. "So you got up after all!"

"I was just telling Marla," his neighbor said, "if you really want to leave the dogs, I'll take care of them. They're no problem."

Michael winked playfully at her.

"I'd rather leave my wife and take you," he grinned, leaning forward to peck at her cheek. Pat and Marla laughed good-naturedly, then Marla pouted with mock offense and climbed into the camper.

"We'd better get started," Michael said, fumbling in the pocket of his sports shirt for his ignition keys. He tipped his buff-colored, narrow-brimmed golfing hat as he headed for the driver's cab. "See you in a couple of weeks, neighbor!" He winked again at Pat. At the door of the driving cab he turned and looked back. Samson was still sitting patiently watching from the front lawn.

"Come on, boy—you're coming with us,

too. Don't look so forlorn," Michael called, and eagerly the dog darted forward and leaped into the camper through the side door. "Okay, you can close it now, honey," Michael yelled to Marla. "And make sure it's good and secure." Then he climbed up into the driver's seat, slammed the cab door and lowered the window slightly. He looked around. Marla had moved up front to the passenger seat beside him and the two children were sitting behind, stroking the dogs.

Pat Parks crossed the street to stand on the sidewalk outside her home as Michael started the engine, put it in first gear and slowly pulled away. Marla returned Pat's wave as they rolled off around the bend.

Pat was about to turn and go back indoors as the camper was disappearing from view, but paused when she saw, heading up the street in the same direction that the Drakes were heading, a long, low, black hearse. She clutched her robe around her involuntarily as it went by. The windows of the hearse were frosted glass and she could not see into the back of the vehicle properly, but she thought she got an impression of a peculiarly bulky coffin lying inside.

Out on Ventura Boulevard there was little traffic and Michael made good time, nosing the camper southeast toward the San Bernardino freeway. Marla was in a happy, joking mood and the children took turns riding up front, sitting between them, placing the bewildered little German shepherd pups on the broad, flat top of the dashboard to give them, as Steve put it, a good view. The children hooted with laughter as the pups stood, wobbly-legged, peering out the windscreen, their attention attracted by every bright object that flashed by. The disturbance of the previous night was totally forgotten. Nor did Michael even notice in his rear-view mirror the black hearse, tailing him at a cautious distance. And even if he had, he would doubtless have thought little of the funeral car's presence, with the holiday mood bubbling happily all around as he drove.

Out on the freeway, the foothills of the Colorados soon appeared in the distance and Michael pointed out their purple, hazy beauty. Soon they were rolling down a gently sloping valley, flanked on either side by the green blur of rich forest, which signaled that they had not far to go to their destination, Lake Arrowhead.

To a psychologist, which was Michael's profession, the lake and its utter peace and freedom represented the ultimate in mental and bodily relaxation, away from the complex pressures created by the city and, to a lesser extent, suburban environment in which people found themselves forced to survive— or succumb. The moment he got out into these patently natural, tranquil surroundings, the mountains of worry and responsibility that his work constantly heaped upon him rolled from the vault of his mind like retreating thunderhead clouds after a tropical storm. Case histories, sociological surveys, files, folders, psychoses and neuroses—all the terms and trappings of his profession were left behind in the environment that had helped create them. Nature was nature—it functioned eternally on its own levels and on its own terms.

It was only early afternoon by the time the paved road leading down to the complex of lakes turned to worn dirt track, and eventually Michael eased the camper onto the uneven grassy banks below which lay one of the largest of the freshwater lakes. He pulled up near a tall, stout-trunked tree whose foliage spread out like an umbrella, on the fringe of the woods. Across the millpond-smooth lake, fishermen lay back in their rowboats, their lines trailing in the water, and beyond, on the opposite bank, rose a steep hillside, dotted with clustered bushes and evergreens.

The only people near Michael's chosen parking spot were a group of campers who appeared to be clearing away their belongings, as if about to move out.

While the children ran and tumbled in the grass, playing with Samson, Annie and the pups, Michael and Marla got out the portable folding table and chairs for a picnic lunch. The pups brought screeches of delighted laughter from Steve and Linda as, for the first time, they learned how to half-climb, half-tumble in and out of their box, clownishly falling head over heels, their short stubby legs paddling the air as they struggled to regain their balance. As the sun rose higher and burned hotter, Michael slid the pups' box under the rear of the camper for protection and assembled a tubular-framed awning over the lunch table. Marla, meanwhile, got to work with her boxes of groceries and the portable stove.

Just before lunch was served their camper-neighbors departed, waving cheerily and wishing them a happy holiday. Then Marla called Steve and Linda to the table. The two dogs sat obediently by, waiting for any left-over scraps that might be tossed to them. And, as a second thought, Steve carried over the pups to feed them morsels. Once more the children were howling with laughter as the tiny bundles of puppy fat tumbled and rolled over backward, legs flailing, in their first attempts to imitate the begging of the two adult dogs.

Helping himself to coleslaw, Michael said, "Well . . . we're in luck! You know, this is *exactly* the same spot we were at last year. And remember? We didn't see more than four people during the entire two weeks!"

"Daddy," said Steve, "can Linda and me sleep outside the camper tonight?"

Marla frowned. "I really don't think so, honey," she said.

Michael spread his hands and shrugged.

"We've got Samson and Annie here and they'd be right outside the camper. We can set the kids up. What's the big deal?"

Steve looked at his mother.

"Please . . . Mom?"

Marla smiled at his persistence, his exaggeratedly wistful expression.

"We'll see," she said, ruffling his hair. Linda was pretending not to be a part of the persuasion plot, garnishing a hamburger generously.

"Are you sure you've had enough of that relish, young lady?" Marla said, taking the jar from her. "You won't be able to taste the *burger*, ladling it on like that."

As the family finished off their lunch and Marla served up coffee for herself and Michael, and milkshakes for the children, the dogs had become temporarily forgotten. Samson had wandered off, surveying his new temporary territory, examining each tree in a wide circle. Annie was sprawled out, dozing, with one of her pups curled beside her. But the other pup had strayed off to do some exploring of his own in this, his first encounter with the real outdoors.

Still wobbly on his feet and slightly uncertain of his balance, the little pup meandered farther and farther away from the campsite, sniffing at the grass, cocking his floppy ears at unfamiliar insect sounds and ambling haphazardly down the grassy bank beneath the trees toward the edge of the lake. An abandoned canoe, its hull slightly holed, lay tethered at the edge of the shallow water, partly hidden in reeds. Curious, the pup placed his paws against the nearest side of the boat, then with a little struggle, squirmed up over the edge and tumbled inside.

By dusk the Drakes had realized the pup was missing and were combing the clumps of bushes around their camp, Steve and Linda calling out concernedly.

"Here, puppy! Here, boy! C'mon now! Here, puppy!"

Marla looked crestfallen and, apologetically, said to Michael quietly, "I'm sorry I agreed to bring the dogs, now. I really didn't think they'd be any bother."

Michael put an arm around her.

"Don't worry about it," he said. "Anyway, there's not much we can do tonight."

"Daddy," Steve called, "I think we'd better tie Annie up for the night or she'll get lost, too!"

He pointed and Michael looked to see Annie wandering about anxiously, sniffing the ground and whimpering, her remaining pup trailing along behind.

Samson was away somewhere in the dis-

Alive with pleasure!

Newport

©Lorillard, U.S.A., 1976

18 mg. "tar", 1.2 mg. nicotine
av. per cigarette, FTC Report Dec. 1976.

Warning: The Surgeon General Has Determined That Cigarette Smoking Is Dangerous to Your Health.

tance, also combing the grass and bushes impatiently and barking occasionally.

"Daddy!" Linda shouted suddenly. "Samson's running off!"

"No he's not, sweetie," Michael reassured her. "He's searching for the pup. Come on, let's get ready for bed. We'll look again in the morning. After all, he's just a *little* puppy —he can't be too far."

He glanced up at the quickly darkening sky and, although he did not show it on his ruggedly handsome face, Michael was more concerned than he had admitted. He glanced across the lake where the sun was setting behind the high hill opposite, then turned to usher the children inside to get ready for bed and prepare their sleeping bags.

Up there on the hill, practically invisible in the rapidly dying light, stood the black hearse that had trailed the Drakes. It was parked near the summit beside some bushes. Alongside it stood the ominous, black-clad figure of Veidt Smit.

Smit waited motionless, zombielike, watching the last traces of the sun die beyond the far mountains, then walked slowly to the rear of the funeral car. He opened the rear, with its frosted glass panel, and inside lay the coffin of Zoltan. Veidt reached inside and lifted off the lid.

Within a moment, the hulk inside began to stir. It rose, stretched, then Zoltan climbed out to jump down and sit beside his master, eyes glinting malevolently once again, now that night had fallen. The dog's fangs were already bared and dripping with saliva, as if in anticipation of its loathsome feasts ahead.

Close at hand came the howling of many wolves. It was almost as if the sound sprang up at the rising of his hand, just as the music of a great orchestra seems to leap under the baton of the conductor . . . As the door began to open, the howling of the wolves without grew louder and angrier; their red jaws, with champing teeth, and their blunt-clawed feet as they leaped, came in through the opening door. I knew then that to struggle at that moment against the Count was useless. With such allies as these at his command, I could do nothing.

—Bram Stoker, *Dracula* (1897)
(The New American Library, 1965)

NINE:

Menace in the Night

The calm waters at the edge of the lake rippled softly against the banks. Cicadas chirped intermittently from the still grass. The Drakes' camper was in darkness, with Steve and Linda warm and sleeping soundly in their sleeping bags just outside the door. Annie and her pup were sleeping, too. But

Samson was not around; he had not returned after wandering off in search of the missing pup.

With a start, Annie came awake and raised her head, ears perked, sniffing the night air. But there was only the sound of the crickets on the tranquil breeze, and the scents of cooling earth.

Down by the lake, the lost puppy was still struggling, whimpering faintly as it vainly tried to climb out of the abandoned canoe. Time and time again it had placed its paws on the inside of the hull and lunged for the upper edge. But the curved hull was too deep, slippery with moss and the slime of water seepage, and the tiny, uncoordinated little creature could not manage a powerful enough leap to gain its freedom. Each time it tried, it slid or tumbled in a furry bundle, back into the damp bottom of the boat.

The pup was about to make yet another effort when a sound made it freeze, listening intently. Then suddenly, over the edge of the canoe reared a hideous head, monstrous, its baleful eyes glaring with a green light, enormous jaws crammed with bared, treacherous fangs. The pup trembled, its whining increasing as the menacing shape moved closer. Then there was one loud, shrill shriek of terror which was cut off instantaneously as the fangs of Zoltan dug sharply into the pup's jugular vein. The pathetic little creature hung there limply in the great hellhound's jaws as its lifeblood was quickly drained. Then Zoltan dropped the slack bundle back to the floor of the canoe with a dull thud. He raised his head to look up at the sky and his fangs were spattered with dripping crimson. The bright full moon intensified the malevolent glints of green fire which were the eyes of the vampire hound.

Back at the camper, Steve and Linda still slumbered soundly, even when a dark shadow cut off the moonlight bathing their faces. Above them, looking down with obscene gluttony, stood the satanic Zoltan, about to strike and claim yet another victim.

A sudden loud barking rasped the night. Zoltan turned his head to see Samson streaking furiously toward him from the direction of the woods. A few feet away, by the camper, Annie also served to startle and unnerve the bloodthirsty hound with her sharp throaty barks, and Zoltan bounded quickly away, running at tremendous speed, shining blackly in the moonlight.

Michael Drake burst out of the caravan and leaped into a kneeling position by the sleeping bags to make sure the children were unharmed. Steve and Linda were blinking themselves awake, puzzledly. Marla was right behind Michael, and after crouching briefly beside him and seeing that the children were all right, she went off to try to quiet Annie, who was still barking wildly and tugging the chain which tethered her to straining point. Michael looked up, squinting into the darkness, swiftly scanning the direction of Samson's barking, and was in time to see his dog disappear behind a clump of bushes, in pursuit of an unnamable gray-black hulk.

Around the edge of the lake the powerful hound tore, its paws throwing up clods of soft earth as it pounded along, with Samson in pursuit. On the far side of the lake, below the hill where Veidt had parked his hearse, was a sealed-off area, protected by a stockadelike enclosure, with thick pointed-topped wooden poles sunk into the ground and flanked on the slope side by coil upon coil of barbed wire. A large sign nailed to the stockade wall read: PRIVATE PROPERTY: NO TRESPASSING. The sturdy fence was almost twenty feet high, yet without hesitation, Zoltan cleared it in one gigantic, flying leap, disappearing in the darkness beyond.

When Samson reached the fence a few moments later, he realized instinctively that he could not make the jump if he tried and, paws splayed, braked to a halt before it, looking up. He sniffed impatiently around at the base of the hefty poles, then followed them around to the barbed-wire barricade at the hillside extremity. By crawling on his belly, catching only tufts of fur on the sharp barbs, he was able to wriggle beneath the wire barrier and gain access to the area behind the stockade and pick up Zoltan's trail again.

By now, Zoltan had reached the summit and stood before Veidt, gazing up at his master's lurking expression of anger and displeasure.

"The only blood we need is the blood of Michael Drake!" Zoltan seemed to hear Veidt say.

Hanging his head, still panting from his race across the lakeside, ears drooping, Zoltan retreated, moving toward the open door of the hearse where his coffin lay. But the lid was closed. The great dog looked inquiringly up at Veidt. A noise of rustling sounded off in the bushes and the man in black stepped forward and quickly held the coffin lid while Zoltan leaped inside, closing it quietly after him. The first tentative streaks of sunlight were beginning to color the eastern sky.

Veidt closed and locked the rear door of the hearse and turned to see a large German shepherd, sniffing the ground, moving closer across the small clearing, as if trying to retrace a lost trail. Samson cocked his ears, listening for any familiar sound as he came up to the hearse and circled it, still sniffing.

Back at the campsite, both Steve and Linda were now wide awake as the first dawnlight appeared beyond the far mountains. They were carefully rolling up their sleeping bags, watched by Michael and

Marla, who frequently looked anxiously around.

"I didn't see *anything*, Mom," Steve was insisting, in answer to Marla's concerned questioning.

"I heard a lot of barking, that's all," Linda said.

As they picked up the rolled bags, Michael began to hustle them toward the open door of the camper. "You kids come inside now," he said. They went in ahead of him and at the door he turned to Marla, looking thoughtful.

"It looked like a big wolf," he said quietly. "But there are no wolves in this area. At least I never heard of any."

"Samson was chasing *something*," Marla said, stabbing nervously at her light auburn hair with a hand. "It could have been a prowler." She hesitated, then said confidingly, "Maybe we ought to move to a trailer camp tomorrow."

Michael looked down at his slippered feet awkwardly, thrusting both hands in the pockets of his robe.

"Aw . . . I don't know, honey," he said. "After all, this is the place we've been looking for—nothing's changed since last year. It'll be all right."

He allowed Marla to enter the trailer ahead of him and paused at the door to glance at Annie, tethered at the corner of the vehicle. She was sitting quietly now, her pup between her forepaws. The light of dawn was turning a faint rose color, sending gentle rays down through the valley surrounding the tranquil waters of the lake.

Beyond, up the hillside, Samson was completing his investigation of the area around the parked black hearse. He looked about him for a final time, sniffing, but the scent he had been following had faded. Ignoring the stock-still, silent figure of Veidt, he turned and loped off down the hill, making for the edge of the lake.

Once the sun rose fully the family, unable to snatch any more sleep after the excitement, breakfasted, and when they had finished, Linda helped her mother with the dishes, while Michael and Steve went off in search of the lost pup. Annie, who was still tethered by the camper, began barking insistently again as they left, her remaining pup staying close by her. When she had finished helping her mother, Linda walked over and stroked Annie, trying to calm her, but the dog was staring out toward the lake excitedly. Linda skipped over to her mother and put on a mournful face.

"Mommy . . . can I help Dad and Steve look for the puppy now?"

Marla brushed a stray lock of hair from Linda's face, then glanced around the lake valley. It all seemed so bright, peaceful and friendly, now that the upsets of the night had gone.

"Okay, honey," she said. "But don't worry —they'll find it."

Linda ran off in the direction that Michael and Steve had headed a few minutes after breakfast. They had separated and were searching among the trees in the wood beyond the camper, calling from time to time for the puppy. Steve gently swished the grass ahead of him with a long thin branch of wood.

Failing to find them immediately, Linda went her own way, heading off along the northern shore of the lake. She wandered along, calling out occasionally, until she came to the high wooden palings with the PRIVATE PROPERTY sign. She would dearly love, she thought, to be the one to find the lost puppy . . . alone and single-handed. It always seemed to be Steve or her father who came out on top and won the day in this sort of situation. She'd love to see their faces if, this time, she went back in triumph to the camper, carrying the pup.

She peered in the gap between two of the wooden palings. There was nothing behind but a grassy slope, rising steeply and dotted with thick clusters of bushes. There didn't seem to be anyone about. And anyway, if anyone did catch her "trespassing," they'd understand when she told them what she was doing there. The only problem was how to get inside the fence.

She slowly made her way along the stockade wall until she reached the precipitous incline where the barbed wire sealed the gap between the fence and the face of the vertical hill. Thre was a gap just large enough for her to squirm through, if she held back the wire with a tree branch. She found one nearby, carefully edged through, trying not to tear her blouse or slacks, and made it to the other side. After searching around at the foot of the steep hill, she began to make her way up the slope.

By the time she reached the top she was almost out of breath. She stepped around a tall, thick clump of bushes and halted. There before her, parked in an almost circular clearing near the summit, was a big, black, long, shiny station wagon, glistening with morning dew. Suddenly, it dawned on her what it was, why it was so big and long and black and creepy-looking. She approached it gingerly . . .

Down beside the lake, Michael and Steve had spotted Samson sniffing about excitedly, making impatient whimpering sounds, near an object at the water's edge among the reeds. Steve ran forward and reached the abandoned canoe before his father. He stood on tiptoe at the water's edge and, momentarily, his face lit up with delight.

"There he is, Daddy!" he called, pointing into the boat and craning his neck to see. Then he saw that the furry little bundle was not moving, and his face fell as the truth occurred to him.

"I think he's dead," Steve said as his father arrived at his side. Michael stepped forward, reached down and gently lifted the limp, fluffy shape from the canoe. He looked quickly at Steve, then, satisfied that the boy was not too upset, began to examine the puppy's body. His superficial search for any signs of injury revealed nothing. Samson barked angrily at his elbow.

"Maybe it was that big wolf you saw last night," Steve said.

Michael took the sagging head of the pup in his hand and looked at its face. Its mouth was open in a grimacing death rictus and its eyes were staring wide. He turned away so that Steve would not see.

"He must have died of exposure," Michael said. With the puppy in one hand, he placed his other arm around the boy's shoulders consolingly and steered him gently away toward the camper. Samson ran alongside, still barking.

"What do you think we should do with him?" Steve asked, nodding toward the dead pup.

"We'll bring him back to camp and bury him around there," Michael said.

Linda jumped, startled, when she suddenly became aware of the figure in black standing by the rear door of the hearse. He seemed to have appeared out of nowhere. She looked at his face. He wore dark glasses and showed no sign of greeting.

"Hi!" she said nervously, still a trifle jumpy and out of breath from her climb up the hill. "My name is Linda Drake and . . . and we're camping down below and we lost our puppy. Have you seen him?"

The tall figure made no reply. He simply stood there gazing at her from behind those eyeless dark lenses.

Linda nodded toward the hearse.

"You have a funeral car, mister," she said, as if attempting to make conversation. Veidt Smit slowly reached up and removed his shades. His eyes were flat, cold and expressionless, like those of a snake.

"He was only four weeks old," Linda went on nervously, everything she said dangling on the air, unacknowledged. She smiled and shrugged self-consciously. "I don't think he could have made it all the way up here." She extended her hand. "Well, thanks anyway, mister!"

Veidt reached out and took her hand. She looked up into his skull-like face and was becoming fascinated by those expressionless yet penetrating eyes when she heard her father's voice from below.

"Linda! Linda, where are you?"

Veidt jerked his hand away hurriedly and replaced his sunglasses.

"Come back!" her father's voice called. "We found the puppy!"

Linda smiled. "They found him!" she said delightedly. "Bye, mister!" She whirled and ran off down the steep hill, grasping on branches to keep her balance.

Veidt stared coldly after her.

Michael dug the shallow hole by a gnarled old tree on the fringe of the wood, as Marla, Steve and Samson stood looking on. Samson continued to bark at irregular intervals. Marla looked back over her shoulder and saw her daughter running down toward the camper.

"Linda! Linda!" she called. "Over here!"

In a few seconds, Linda was only a few yards away, breathless. Before she could join them, Marla stepped forward a few paces, knelt before her and took her by the shoulders.

"I'm sorry, honey," she said, as sympathetically as she could. "The pup was dead . . . in an abandoned canoe."

Suddenly, all the eagerness went out of Linda's eyes. She shook her head and sighed, looking back toward the camper.

"Poor Annie . . ." she said, stifling a sob.

Marla took her hand and led her among the little group gathered around the small hole in the ground. Michael was holding the dead puppy. Steve handed him a pillow case he had brought along.

"Thanks," Michael said. "We'll just wrap him up in this."

"Sure, Dad," said Steve, attempting to sound matter-of-fact and manly, now that Linda was here.

"I know where there's a funeral car," Linda said abstractedly, but no one took any notice.

As Michael began to slip the puppy's body into the pillow case, he felt something damp on his fingers. He looked and saw slight smears of blood. Shielding what he was doing from the others, he carefully inspected the puppy's head and neck. With his fingers, he parted the fur and in the flesh of the neck beneath saw two small incisions, encircled with clotted blood. Marla saw him frowning.

"What's wrong?" she asked.

"Nothing." He shrugged. "I think a rattler got him."

He finished wrapping the pup in the pillow case, then crouched to lay it gently in the shallow grave. He took the spade from Steve and slowly shoveled the soil over the pathetic little white bundle. Handing the spade back to Steve, he took out a cloth and wiped the smears of blood and traces of soil from his hands. Then he turned and slipped an arm around his wife's waist and another around Linda's shoulders and began to lead them back toward the campsite. Steve marched along beside them with the spade.

Samson, who had fallen silent, lingered behind. He went forward to the little patch of turned earth, sniffed at it for a moment, then turned and ran off to follow the family.

All day, the children were noticeably silent, toying moodily with their food and showing no desire to play about the camp, or with the dogs, or do anything in particular. Understandably, the finding of the dead puppy had upset them, but neither Michael nor Marla attempted in any way to dispel their dampened spirits. Without anything actually being said, they intuitively realized that perhaps it was best to let the mood disperse of its own accord. A good night's sleep —this time *inside* the camper—and they would no doubt be back in a happier, lighter frame of mind by the morning.

That night Steve and Linda went quietly, unprotestingly to bed in their bunks within the camper. Shortly after eleven, Michael and Marla retired, too.

The full moon lay reflected in the lake and threw its bright silver beams over the halftones of the woods and grassy slopes. Once again cicadas and night insects set up their continuous chorus. Out by the gnarled old tree, there eventually came a much fainter, more unusual sound. Beneath the low, circular mound of earth where the family had buried the puppy, there was a persistent scratching noise, like that of some burrowing creature. It grew more and more agitated until eventually, the soil around the top of the mound began to undulate and crumble away. Then, out from the earth stirred a whitish shape, coated in damp deposits of mud, which wriggled and writhed until from it struggled the tiny head of the Drake's puppy. The little creature struggled for a moment to free its back legs, then crawled unsteadily forward, away from the mound. As the moonlight fell upon the animal's face, its eyes were dull and vacant, yet open wide, almost as they had appeared in death. Slowly, it half-stumbled, half-crawled into the undergrowth of the forest.

Dhampir is the Serbian name for a vampire's son . . . [He] was far from faithful to his parent and was quite happy, in return for some kind of settlement, to exterminate father . . . and the last known *dhampir* activity was recorded in 1959 at Vrbrica, a village in the province of Kosovo-Metohija.

—Anthony Masters, *The Natural History of the Vampire* (Putnam, 1972)

TEN:

Look Terror in the Face

Zoltan stood facing his master, head raised, ears forward and alert, as if listening intently. The cold, compelling eyes of Veidt Smit bore down into those of the mesmerized hound as Veidt burned his thoughts into the dog's enslaved brain.

"Get help," the sibilant voice of Veidt's inner self commanded. "We are going to need some help."

Zoltan bared his fangs and growled, low and hollow in his chest, his green-lit eyes burning.

100

"Go!" hissed the voice, and Zoltan sprang off into the night.

Jo Jo Levene and Harry Sim had had another good day's fishing. They had dined well on their catch and, as usual, had curled up under the stars in their sleeping bags. Thanks to the beer with which they had washed down their supper, leaving empty cans scattered around their little campsite, they slumbered soundly, snoring heartily and rhythmically. At their feet were stacked their fishing baskets, rods, nets and lines, and beyond that, Sim's black-and-white-spotted hound dog, Buster, lay beside the fading embers of the campfire, with one eye open. Down through the woods behind their camp, the dark hulk of Zoltan moved stealthily through the trees. He came to the edge of the clearing where they lay and stood, surveying the scene. It was not long before Buster, lying downwind of the lurking predator, picked up his scent and jumped up, barking, running toward the shadowy shape in the foliage. Zoltan wheeled and bounded off up the forest slopes with Buster on his heels.

The noise of the barking awakened Jo Jo and his partner, and the two men sat up in their sleeping bags, grimacing, trying to peer around them into the darkness and to shake the alcoholic haze of sleep from their heads. Jo Jo rubbed his weatherworn face with his hands and drew the back of one hand over his drooping black mustache. He looked over at Sim, who was stretching his square jaw in a wide yawn.

"Hey!" he said in a hoarse whisper. "Your dog's nuts!" Sim looked over.

"He's supposed to be a watch dog," Jo Jo went on, "and all he does is scare the hell out of us!"

Sim stretched his powerful, muscular arms and shoulders and scratched his bushy salt-and-pepper curls with a ham of a hand.

"There's one thing I know about Buster," he said, indignantly. "He don't get that excited over nothin'. Whatever he's chasing wasn't supposed to be here."

Jo Jo lay back, abandoning his struggle to awaken properly, and began to pull his blanket over his head.

"Yeah, sure," he murmured with sarcasm. "Tomorrow he'll be chasing *us*."

Sim snorted in disdain, turned over and went back to sleep.

Zoltan darted up through the woods with Buster slowly gaining upon him as they wove in and out through the trees. Buster was still barking furiously. Higher and higher the dogs climbed until, a few yards after they burst out of the heavy underbrush, the leading dog stopped abruptly in his tracks, whirled, sat on his haunches and faced the oncoming pursuer. When he saw Zoltan's about-face, Buster halted, too, a few feet away, puzzled by the intruder's action. For seconds the two dogs faced each other across a bed of forest leaves and damp soil, glaring into each other's faces, neither of them giving ground, nor moving a muscle. Gradually, Buster began to be mesmerized by the baleful, vine-green eyes of the monstrous dog sitting bolt upright before him. Slowly, his eyes still boring into those of Buster, Zoltan rose, moving only his legs and body, keeping the plane of his glance perfectly steady and directly riveted upon the black-and-white hound dog. Buster did not move, but simply kept staring glassily ahead, even when Zoltan moved out of his range of vision to stand towering beside him.

Then, the mighty, gray-black devil-dog bared its fangs and, swift as a striking cobra, sank them into the hunting dog's neck. Still Buster stood there passively, putting up not even the faintest struggle, nor even making a murmur as Zoltan lapped his blood. After a few moments, Zoltan stepped back a pace and walked slowly on up the slope, his jaws running red. Buster got up and followed a few paces behind, as if in a deep hypnotic trance.

Zoltan led Buster up the hill until they reached the small clearing where Veidt waited beside the black funeral limousine. Zoltan approached his master and gazed into his face, while Buster sat down nearby, patiently. The sinister figure looked down at

Zoltan briefly, then his sluggish, dead eyes turned to study the new recruit that his charge had brought before him. The black-and-white dog no longer had the appearance of the trusty guard and hunting companion of Harry Sim. His ears were drawn back, giving him a permanently menacing expression, his eyes now glinted the same unholy green as Zoltan's, and from his mouth protruded an unnaturally pronounced set of teeth, particularly the ultra-large, razor-sharp canines.

Veidt's expressionless living-corpse face give no hint of his satisfaction with Zoltan's choice of a partner. He simply switched his gaze back to Zoltan and, employing his extra-sensory powers as before, ordered:

"Take him with you."

Without hesitation, Zoltan turned to face Buster and, his face in a commanding snarl, growled low and menacingly. Then he moved off unhurriedly toward the woods, and within seconds, Buster followed obediently behind.

The white gloss of the Drake camper stood out gleaming starkly in the bright moonlight against the duller tones of the surrounding grass and forest. In file, the two malevolent vampire dogs emerged from the wooded shadows and headed determinedly for the Drake's mobile home. The lights were out.

A few yards from the vehicle, Zoltan stopped until Buster came up beside him. He gave his new comrade a long, piercing look, using his uncanny powers to open his mind and allow Buster to read his intentions. After a few moments, Buster walked on alone toward the camper, while Zoltan lay crouched, looking on.

Almost as if he were a ghost, Buster glided silently by the sleeping forms of Drake's two German shepherds and their pup without waking them. He reached the camper door and, rearing up on his hind legs, grasped the stainless-steel handle gently in his jaws, pressing downward. The door opened soundlessly.

Past the two children slumbering in their bunk beds the large dog padded silently, looking almost phosphorescent in the rays of the moon that streaked in through the window. Cold night air from the open door wafted into the camper. Beside Michael Drake's bunk, Buster squatted on his haunches, peeling back his lips, baring his savage teeth as he eyed his intended victim. Michael slept on, unaware.

But the chilly draft from the door blew on the face of young Steve and made him stir uncomfortably. He opened his eyes. He immediately saw the large, whitish shape crouching menacingly beside his father's sleeping form.

"Dad!" he yelled at the top of his voice.

Instantly, Michael Drake sprang up from his pillow as the big black-spotted hound made a lunge at him. But the sharp cry of the boy and Michael's sudden movement made the dog falter and miss its target, and, startled, it turned and bolted out of the door.

Outside, Samson and Annie barked deafeningly and constantly in the ensuing uproar.

"What's happening?" Marla shrieked as Michael, now out of bed, dug beneath the pillow for his revolver.

"Stay put, Marla!" he shouted. "Keep the children inside!" And he burst out the door.

Gun held before him, ready to shoot, steadying it with his left hand on right wrist, Michael swiftly darted a glance around. He saw the white shape of the fleeing dog in the distance, with Samson in hot pursuit. He aimed his gun, but the distance was too great for accuracy, and he did not want to take the risk of hitting Samson by mistake. As he lowered the gun, frowning, the light went on in the camper behind him and Marla appeared in the doorway, the two children sheltering at her back in the folds of her robe.

Just then an enormous black shape came hurtling, as if from nowhere, and was upon him. Marla screamed as her husband was flung to the ground by great clubbed paws by a gargantuan black animal that snarled and roared more loudly than a mountain lion.

Michael was on his back on the earth, the giant form of Zoltan pinioning him to the ground under its crushing weight. The creature's jaws gaped above his face, dripping and blasting his nostrils with a hideous, sickening stench. And its roaring, snarling hatred almost deafened him. As they struggled, Michael flailing his arms to try to fight off the loathsome beast, he looked for the first time directly into the terrifying face of the hound from hell; the beast which, although he did not know it, had traveled halfway across the world with Veidt Smit, to make him their new master.

As they rolled from side to side on the damp earth, Zoltan also looked directly down upon his intended victim. For a split second, man and hound stared full at each other. Then, without warning, Zoltan's eyes dilated horribly. He threw back his head and gave out an unnerving, ear-splitting shriek of fear. The dog leaped off its struggling, pinioned prey and, with huge bounds, raced away.

Michael rolled quickly to his feet. He looked after the still-whining, howling creature amazedly, then, instinctively, he raised his revolver, took careful aim and fired three times. He stared after the apparition unbelievingly as its cries and weird luminescent bulk disappeared, still running like the wind.

Marla and the children rushed over to him and hugged him, shaking with fear, more terrified, in fact, than Michael appeared to be.

"Are you all right, darling?" Marla sobbed.

"I'm . . . fine," Michael gasped, clutching his trembling wife and children to him. He panted for a few moments, trying to regain his breath, then said exasperatedly, "I . . . I

could have sworn I hit that animal . . . three
times!" He turned, looking into the wide,
scared and bewildered eyes of his wife, and
shook his head. "I don't get it," he said. "I
just don't get it!"

He crouched down, putting an arm about
each of the pale, shivering children.

"It's okay now, kids," he said quietly. "It's
all over now and Daddy's all right. Okay?"

"But . . . what's it all about?" Marla said,
still looking around fearfully. Michael stood
up.

"I don't know," he breathed, shrugging. "I
guess there's a bunch of wild dogs around."
He hugged her reassuringly. "I'm gonna call
the sheriff's office in the morning and make a
full report."

Despite the chill of the night and the cold-
ness of the damp earth, Michael discovered
that he was bathed in a light film of perspiration. His pajama jacket was shredded
and barely hung from his shoulders.

"Come on," he said, ushering his family
inside. As they trooped back in, Samson returned, panting heavily. Michael paused at
the door and pointed to where Annie still
stood protectively over her pup at the corner
of the camper. She was staring off in the direction the attackers had gone.

"Good boy," Michael said. "Lie down over
there, now. You too, Annie."

He pulled the camper door closed and
flicked the inside catch. Marla was tucking

the children back in their bunks. He went into the bathroom, switched on the light and began to splash cold water in his face. He toweled himself dry, then surveyed himself in the mirror, running a hand through his ruffled, wiry black hair. He did not realize it, but the silver crucifix dangling from a chain about his neck, hanging there at his chest among the torn shreds of his pajama jacket, had just saved his life.

The vampire bat . . . can fly, walk, dodge swiftly, turn somersaults, all with swiftness and efficiency. Generally it attacks cattle rather than men. The victim is not awakened during the attack.

—Raymond T. McNally and Radu Florescu, *In Search of Dracula* (Warner Books, 1973)

ELEVEN:

An Inspector Calls

Vaclav Branco stepped onto the tarmac at Los Angeles International Airport and squinted in the bright sun as he waited in line to board the airline shuttle bus to the terminal building. He clutched a small suitcase and told himself that perhaps even his lightweight tweed suit—with the jacket cut in his favorite Norfolk style—was too heavy for the summer climate of California. However, his matching Homburg—another essential item of his personal preference as part of his "uniform"—would at least serve to keep the sun off his head and neck. His distinctive dress and distinguished, gray-bearded features had earned him plenty of photographic space in Europe's leading magazines and newspapers over the years, so much so that he felt almost duty-bound to maintain a recognizable image.

Ensemble, however, was of the least importance on a grave and urgent assignment such as this. He had already been delayed for far too long. Despite Major Hessle's added influence, red tape had held up the issue of his visa and he had been forced to sit by impatiently in Bucharest until the required officials signed and stamped and approved in triplicate the required documents. All, of course, accompanied by the usual time-wasting officiousness. Of course, had he been in the diplomatic service, or a spy, or a political delegate, it would no doubt have been a mere formality. But to get permission to travel to America to track down a vampire! Try telling that to the closed-minded upstarts at the visa bureau, let alone to a committee of commissars. In the end, his documents had, on the advice of Major Hessle, been made out to appear as if Branco were off on one of his educational/cultural jaunts again, lecturing to criminologists in major West Coast cities.

There was one consolation. His travel agents had assured him that a drive-it-yourself car would be at his disposal immediately on his arrival in Los Angeles.

In fact, within a mere ten minutes of clearing customs, Branco was sitting behind the wheel of a brand-new black Pontiac convertible, heading out toward the L.A. suburb of Tarzana, where, he prayed, Michael Drake still lived. Branco had saved some more time by studying a street map of Greater Los Angeles for about an hour before his flight landed.

It took him only half an hour in the multilane freeway traffic before he was wheeling the car, its roof down, into Kittridge Street, and braking to a halt outside the Drake residence. The large comfortable white house with its spacious gardens was impressive in the eyes of the European visitor.

He walked down the drive and knocked on the door. No answer. He range the bell. No answer. The place sounded empty, in the way that houses often do. He glanced anxiously up at the windows, hoping perhaps that a maid or a house cleaner might be upstairs at work. He knocked again and waited and was about to inspect the rear of the premises when a woman's voice from behind him said:

"Can I help you?"

Branco turned to see a smartly dressed, attractive young woman approaching down the drive.

"Aren't the Drakes in?" he asked, tipping his hat. "I'm . . . an old friend. My name is Branco."

"I'm Mrs. Parks. I'm afraid you missed them by a few days."

"Oh?"

"They're on vacation. They'll be gone a couple of weeks." She studied the obviously European caller, trying to guess the origin of his faint accent. He looked earnestly at her, as if hoping she would proffer more helpful information. Pat Parks smiled.

"I was supposed to take care of their dogs," she said, "but they took the whole brood with them—even the puppies."

"Would you know where they went . . . please?" Branco asked.

"All I can tell you is they're somewhere around the shores of Lake Arrowhead," Mrs. Parks said.

"Any particular hotel or inn?"

She smiled wryly.

"Who can afford hotels? They have their own camper."

"Camper?" The inspector looked puzzled for a moment. Then he said, "Oh yes, I know what they are. . . . Could you give me an idea where they could be?"

"Well, I know Michael was hoping to stay where they went last year. Kind of an isolated spot. Away from any trailer camps."

"Where was that?" He certainly was persistent, this old friend, Mrs. Parks thought.

"I can't tell you exactly," she said, "but I know it's past Clear Lake and before Big Bear. Would you care to leave me your name and where you can be reached in case they come back before you've found them?"

113

"Er . . . no, there'll be no need for that, Mrs. Parks," the Inspector said quickly. "Thank you so much."

He touched his hat and headed off toward his car.

"Mr. Branco?" Mrs. Parks called. "Is there something wrong?"

"Nothing at all, I'm . . . just anxious to find them."

With a wave, Branco climbed into the car and pulled away. At his first stop for gas, Branco inquired directions to Lake Arrowhead and was delighted to be given a free map of the area and to be shown by a station attendant exactly which routes to take.

He peeled off his jacket, rolled up his shirt sleeves, loosened his tie, and got back into his car. If service like that was what was meant in the East by decadence, he thought, Europe could use some of it.

Branco pulled into the parking area beside the Lake Arrowhead Sheriff's Station by late afternoon and found the sheriff, a soft-spoken man of about fifty-four, prone to patting a large paunch that had been developed through a diet of too many burgers, Cokes and shakes. He was, however, eager to help all he could.

"They're somewhere between Clear Lake and Big Bear, I am told," Branco explained. "Could you give me any ideas, Sheriff?"

Sheriff Larsen took off his cap and scratched the top of his head.

"I wish I could," he said. "Problem is, there's still a lot of people camping around, even though the season's nearly over."

"What do you suggest?"

"Well . . . just keep driving along the shore and keep asking. From what you tell me—that camper with all those dogs—I'll bet somebody spotted them."

Branco nodded, then as an afterthought, said, "By the way, can you recommend a place I can stay in for a few nights?" If he didn't find the Drakes quickly, he was ill equipped to spend a night out on the lakeshore.

"Charley's," the sheriff said simply. "If he hasn't closed up for the season yet. His cabins aren't much, but they're clean. North end of the lake. You can't miss his sign."

The inspector smiled.

"You are most kind, Sheriff."

He went out of the station office, got into his car and set off on his camp-to-camp inquiries.

. . . I heard as if from down below in the valley the howling of many wolves. The Count's eyes gleamed and he said:—

"Listen to them—the children of the night. What music they make!" Seeing, I suppose, some expression in my face strange to him, he added:—

"Ah, sir, you dwellers in the city cannot enter into the feelings of the hunter."

—Bram Stoker, *Dracula* (1897)
(The New American Library, 1965)

TWELVE:

Call of the Uncanny

The long, rising, eldritch howl in the distance cut through the night stillness, echoing down along the valley. Beneath the Drakes' camper lay Samson, Annie and the pup. Annie, head on paws, opened her eyes at the eerie, far-off noise, but Samson and the pup remained sleeping. Again the howl rang out, long and high and ending in a descending whine, like some nether-region call to arms. Annie lifted her head, rose up on her fore-paws, stretching, and looked down at her sleeping pup, lying between herself and Samson. She got up and slowly padded away in the direction of the continuing howls.

Inside the camper, all were asleep but Linda. She, too, had been awakened from a listless, superficial sleep by the distant baying noises. She sat up and parted the curtains on the wall beside her lower bunk and looked out, to see Annie wandering away toward the woods. As quietly as she could, glancing around at the rest of the slumbering family, she slid out of bed, into her robe and loafers, and went to the door. She gently eased it open and stared after the receding figure of Annie. Her forehead creased in a childish, determined frown. She closed the door silently behind her and began to run after Annie. But as she followed, Annie began suddenly to bound along hurriedly, and although she ran as fast as she could, Linda realized that she had no chance of catching up.

"Annie! Annie!" she called, but she had lost sight of the dog in the shadows of the trees ahead. A little frightened, Linda looked back, then kept running, hoping that Annie would hear her calls and wait for her.

Annie was way ahead, darting agilely through the trees, oblivious of the girl's cries, spurred on only by the howling, which was growing closer. As she approached the far edge of the woods, the canine wailing ceased and Annie bounded into a clearing, halting abruptly with a bark of surprise. She growled, head thrust forward, lowered, then fell silent.

Before her, sitting side by side on their haunches, were Zoltan and Buster, the two vampire dogs, both staring at her with gleaming, hypnotic gazes. She looked from one to the other, then focused her attention on the larger of the two, Zoltan. She became transfixed as the massive hound's eyes seemed to grow steadily larger and larger. She could not have seen from where she sat, but behind the thick clump of bushes beyond the two dogs, Veidt Smit stood beside his black hearse, concentrating, forcing his own will upon her, via his gray-black hound.

Zoltan continued to stare fixedly into Annie's eyes, feeling the invisible current of his master's command coursing through his brain. Then came the unspoken order:

"Now!"

Zoltan leaped forward and, as Annie stood riveted to the spot, clamped his jaws upon the neck of the German shepherd bitch, sinking his fangs into her jugular vein. Just then Linda burst into the little clearing and shrieked Annie's name, waving her arms fearfully, trying in her terrified way to chase off the huge, gray-black creature locked upon her dog's throat. With a savage snarl, Buster hurled himself at her. Linda stumbled backward, losing her balance, and fell to the ground. As she did so her robe tore and was left hanging in the clamped-shut jaws of the big black-and-white hunting dog. Zoltan turned from his feasting at Annie's neck and glared, snarling, ready to move in with Buster upon the helpless girl.

The sharp crack and echoing boom of two gunshots suddenly rang out, blasting the air, and the two dogs stopped dead in their tracks. Through the trees came the two fishermen, Jo Jo and Sim, carrying rifles, Jo Jo's still smoking at the breech. Seeing the two incredibly fierce and ugly hounds leering, their lips torn back in angry snarls, Sim fired his rifle twice over their heads. Then, startled, he recognized one of the dogs as his own.

"Buster! Come!" he yelled. "Buster! Damn it, come!"

But Zoltan and Buster turned and bounded off into the woods, followed quickly by Annie. Jo Jo ran forward to the fallen girl, who was lying curled up in a bundle in her nightgown, hands over her face in sheer fright. He took her up in his arms.

"Are you all right, honey?" he said anxiously. "Did they hurt you?"

Linda shook her head, her body shaking with uncontrollable sobbing.

Sim was still staring off into the darkness after the dogs.

"I'll be a son of a bitch!" he said, almost to himself, incredulously. "Buster's never acted that way before."

"Come on, Sim," Jo said, walking off with

Linda in his arms. "Pick up my rifle there, will you? We'd better find out where this little lady's come from."

Sim retrieved Jo Jo's rifle from the ground where he had left it when he picked up the girl and followed his partner into the woods, heading back toward the lake.

Samson spotted the two fishermen as they approached the camper. He jumped up and ran toward them, barking furiously. Lights went on in the camper and Michael and his wife ran out, following the dog, shouting. As Samson was about to jump the two men, Michael yelled:

"Down, boy!"

Marla rushed toward Jo Jo, having seen the small figure in his arms.

"My God, it's Linda!" she cried to Michael. "What's happened?"

"Linda! Where were you?" Michael called angrily, struggling to hold back Samson, who was pulling forward, still growling at the two men.

"This your daughter, mister?" Jo Jo said. Linda was still trembling and sniffling quietly in his arms. "She told us we'd find you here."

"Who are you?" Michael demanded angrily.

"My pal and I, we were looking for our dog," Jo Jo explained amiably. "We got to a clearing in the woods just in time."

"A big black dog and my bird dog were

about to rip her apart," Sim said, then added matter-of-factly, "we scared 'em off."

Michael looked at his daughter.

"Linda—why did you leave the camper like that?"

She sniffed and, chokingly through her sobs, managed to speak.

"I . . . woke up from that . . . howling and . . . and saw Annie outside. I chased her but she wouldn't come. She ran away . . . with all those dogs."

Michael glanced suspiciously at Sim.

"What does your dog look like?" he demanded.

"He's an old bird dog," Sim said, thoughtfully, rubbing his wide jaw. "His coat is white with black spots. Except for his paws—they're black and gray."

"I can't understand it," Jo Jo put in. "Buster's a hell of a watch dog. When Sim called him, he didn't even pay attention. Acted like he didn't know him."

Michael looked at Marla.

"That sounds like the same dog who came into our camp last night and jumped me!" he said.

"Buster wouldn't do that!" Sim protested. "That's crazy!"

"Where are you camping?" Michael asked.

"Half a mile down the lake," Jo Jo said, gently lifting Linda down to her feet. Marla stood by and she fell into the warm folds of her mother's robe.

"That area is just about the nicest we've found," Jo Jo added. "Never had any trouble there before."

Michael was about to speak when a series of ear-piercing, spine-chilling howls rent the air and echoed across the lake. Everyone froze. Marla shuddered uncomfortably.

"That's the howl I heard, Daddy!" Linda said excitedly. "That's the same howl . . ."

The group looked at each other nervously. Beside them, Samson tensed, his ears pricked up, listening. The howls came again. Without warning, Samson sprang away and ran wildly off in the direction of the woods.

"Samson!" Michael yelled. "Samson, come back!"

But the dog paid no attention. He was hurtling through the trees. He had recognized one of the howling dogs' voices. It was Annie, his mate.

For the first time, Michael inexplicably felt an uncanny sense of fear gripping him. He looked around at the tense faces, and somehow he sensed they were all in very grave danger.

"Come on, honey," he said with weary exasperation. "We'd all better get back inside."

A person bitten by a rabid dog would, after an incubation period of a month or two, be seized by violent symptoms and almost invariably die an agonizing death.

—Isaac Asimov, *Asimov's Guide to Science*, Vol. 2: *The Biological Sciences* (Pelican Books, 1975)

THIRTEEN:

Last of the Draculas

"I know what you're thinking," Michael said, helping Marla fold up the collapsible picnic table. She looked drawn and worried.

"How can we leave without the dogs?" she said. "It'll break the children's hearts."

"I'm not worried about the dogs," Michael said. "I just want to get us home. Vacation's over."

Marla sighed resignedly. Behind them, Linda and Steve were pottering about, helping to clear up the campsite. The pup had been kept overnight in the camper. Now Steve was retrieving the box from beneath the camper and carrying it inside.

"I can't believe Samson and Annie just disappearing," Marla said. "Especially Annie, leaving her pup behind."

They had gone over and over the same ground during the night, after they had seen the children safely to bed. Michael was not prepared to have his family hang around with a pack of wild dogs on the loose, especially when they seemed to have some strange influence on other dogs. Marla tried to argue that everything would be all right, they would all be safe, that none of this might have happened if everyone had stayed inside the camper at night with the door locked. But, as Michael had pointed out, the door had been locked and yet Linda had gone off on her own, following Annie, without saying a word to anyone.

Marla then tried to appeal to Michael's own considerations: he needed the vacation, the relaxation from his job; it was his favorite spot. Surely the local sheriff could do something about hunting down those dangerous dogs out there?

But Michael was not prepared to have his wife and children sit around and wait until something was done—however much he needed the holiday. At length, he had persuaded her, with one simple argument.

Dogs, he told her, carry rabies. They were notorious for it. Rabies was horrible: tetanus, lockjaw, convulsions, pain, agony . . . death, even. Did she want that to happen to herself or her children? Those dogs out there, if they were carriers, they had only to scratch someone or something to transmit the disease. Didn't she read the papers or anything?

He went on, painting such a horrific picture of the spread and effects of rabies that Marla almost felt guilty about having suggested they stay in the first place. Of course they would pack up and leave as soon as possible the following day.

Now, having slept on it, she was having second thoughts, bringing in fresh arguments.

The sun was out on the lake and everything seemed nice and peaceful and hunkydory again. For Marla, the sunshine had swept away all the fears and anxieties of the night.

But deep within him, Michael felt intuitively that there was something far more serious and threatening happening out there than a pack of wild dogs stalking the neighborhood. He could not imagine what. All he knew was that he had to get his family out, before whatever it was emerged from the shadows.

He stacked four folding chairs together and was about to carry them into the camper when a black convertible pulled off the dirt road over on the ridge to the northwest and came bumping over the grassy slope down toward their camp. He propped the chairs against the outside of the trailer and watched it drawing closer. It pulled up a few yards away and the bearded man in the Homburg at the wheel smiled at him broadly. Michael racked his brains, trying to figure out if he ought to recognize him.

The stranger came over, a triumphant cat-that-got-the-goldfish look on his face.

"You," he said, "are Michael Drake!"

"Why . . . yes," Michael said, puzzled. "How did you know?"

The inspector held out his hand.

"My name is Branco."

He shook Michael's hand warmly, and as Marla and the children wandered curiously over, he tipped his hat, smiling, and introduced himself to them also. Then he glanced around at the neatly cleared site.

"Are you cutting your vacation short?" he asked.

Michael raised a quizzical eyebrow. The inspector laughed.

"Uh . . . your neighbor, Mrs. Parks, told me you'd be gone for two weeks."

Somehow, despite his faintly mocking mysteriousness, Michael was quite taken by the stranger's warm, friendly manner.

"Mr. Branco," he said, smiling, "you seem to know quite a bit about me."

Branco's eyes creased into a good-natured smile in return.

"Any particular reason you were looking for me?" Michael asked.

"I have much to tell you," Branco said. "We both come from the same country." He glanced around at the rest of the family, then, laying a hand on Michael's arm, added, "May I impose on a few minutes of your time before you leave?"

"Well, I do want to pull out of here," Michael said hesitantly.

"It'll only take a few minutes."

Michael thought for a moment, then looked at Marla.

"Honey, I'll be right back," he said.

She nodded slowly, puzzled. Michael and Branco wandered off toward the edge of the lake out of earshot, the inspector gesticulating as he spoke. She watched for several minutes as they passed by the lakeside, obviously deeply engrossed in some serious conversation. After a while, she turned to finish tidying up the camper, ready to be off.

Michael crouched down at the water's edge and, preoccupied, began idly tossing pebbles into the shallows.

"I can still remember the fear and the anger of the crowd in the old country," he was saying. "They told me much later that I was brought out as a child because of a local popular uprising against the bourgeois, that I was evacuated here for my own safety. I guess I'm lucky to be alive." He smiled sadly. "So what's the latest about my notorious family?"

"Well," said Branco, "when the tomb collapsed, we cremated all the Draculas, but two

of the coffins were empty. We called in Major
Hessle, a military archaeologist. Together, we
identified one of the missing corpses as a
fractional lamia."

"What's *that?*" Michael asked.

Branco leaned closer, confidingly.

"A creature who is only part vampire," he
said. He pointed a finger at Michael's chest.
"Your great-great-great-grandfather used him
as his servant. Major Hessle identified him as
a Veidt Smit, from an inscription in the tomb.
The inscription said he died back in the late
seventeenth century, but he may, of course,
have been active on different occasions since
then, revived by various successive masters.
While a stake will prevent a vampire from
stalking again, if someone happens to remove
the stake . . ." Branco shrugged. Then he
added, "We think Smit is after you."

Michael looked up.

"But why?"

"Obviously to turn you into another master he can serve," Branco said. "You are the
last of the line."

Michael looked down at his hands, trying
to assimilate all that the inspector had told
him. It sounded so ludicrous, and yet . . .

"Has anything . . . unusual . . . been happening to you since you came here?" Branco
asked.

"Unusual!" Michael glared up at the Inspector. "Hell, that's why we're getting out
of this area."

"What do you mean?"

"The first night some big black dog nearly scared us to death. The next night *two* of them attacked us. Last night our little girl wandered off and some fishermen actually saved her from being torn to bits by another pack—or maybe it was the same pack, I don't know."

"What about *your* two dogs?" Branco inquired.

"That's another thing," Michael said. "They're gone. Haven't seen 'em since last night. I was about to report all this to the sheriff."

"And did you?"

"Not yet."

"Good!" said the Inspector. "Mr. Drake, only you and I can understand. We never could convince the police of anything like this."

Michael nodded noncommittally.

"Then what do we do?"

The inspector caught his eyes and looked directly into them.

"We have to dispose of Smit," he said.

"What?" Michael arched his eyebrows unbelievingly.

"It's either him or you and your family," the Inspector said earnestly. "And God knows how many more."

"But . . . how can you find him . . . if what you tell me is true?"

129

"You forget," Branco said. "He wants your blood. He'll come to you!"

Michael thought hard. It still seemed so incredible. For a fleeting moment, he wondered if maybe the inspector wanted to use him as bait to trap some ordinary criminal, perhaps someone who was wanted for extradition. But if that were so, why go to all these great lengths about vampires and part vampires and so on? Besides, he *had* heard stories . . . about the Dracula family and the old country beliefs.

"I will help you," Branco said, seeing his hesitation. "You and I will stay put. Your wife and children must go home. I have rented a cabin nearby. And I know what to do."

Michael thought it over. If what Branco said was true, then he was duty-bound to try to stop the spread of the vampire plague here in his adopted country. If not and this Smit fellow was an ordinary human criminal, then he had comparatively little to fear. And staying around, he might even stand a chance of getting the dogs back. He looked up at the Inspector, then rose to his feet and nodded. Branco pumped his hand gratefully and they walked back up the slope toward the camper.

High up on the hill on the opposite side of the lake, Veidt Smit was watching the two figures moving toward the Drake camper.

Even at such a distance, it was not difficult to recognize the distinctive figure of Inspector Vaclav Branco. Smit's eyes narrowed with loathing and his mouth tightened into a grim slit.

There are four types of vampire bat although there is little distinction between them: the *Desmodus rufus*, the *Didemus yungi*, the *Diphylla caudata*, and the *Desmodus rotunda*. All are blood-sucking, all spread rabies and in the main all attack cattle and horses, biting them on the neck.

—Anthony Masters, *The Natural History of the Vampire* (Putnam, 1972)

Their bite has an anaesthetic quality and their saliva an anti-coagulating property which facilitates the flow of blood from the wounds they inflict . . .

—Ornella Volta, *The Vampire* (Tandem Books, 1965)

FOURTEEN:

Siege at Charley's

Marla was at the wheel of the big white camper with the window down, looking at Michael standing outside. Steve and Linda were hanging out of one of the side windows. They were parked at a junction of the access road leading onto the freeway. Behind

Michael, waiting in the convertible with the engine still running, sat Inspector Branco.

"Can you trust this man?" Marla said, with a note of finality.

"*I* trust him," Michael said. "And you must trust *me*. I'll be back as soon as I can."

Marla sighed frustratedly.

"Why don't you call the police?"

"Marla, quit worrying," Michael said quietly. "This is something I've got to do on my own. I'll explain everything when I get home."

Linda called out from her windowseat perch, "Daddy, you be sure you find Samson and Annie!"

That's what he'd had to tell the children; that he was staying on to try to get the dogs back. It was the only thing he *could* say that they would understand.

"I want to stay with you, Daddy," Steve called imploringly.

"You take care of your mother, Steve," Michael said.

He reached up and kissed his wife goodbye. Marla tried to smile, but it froze only half-formed on her face. She dabbed at her eyes as Michael walked down the camper to kiss the children through the window, then he turned his back to join Branco in the waiting car.

They doubled back on the mountain road as the camper moved off toward the freeway. Branco steered the Pontiac steadily along the winding narrow curve past the site where the Drakes had been camped and on up toward the north end of the lake. Soon, he pulled off the road and down a dirt track to a small, run-down summer cabin, whose windows were both on the front. A sign nailed to a nearby pine tree said: CHARLEY'S. There were more cabins, farther along the lake, all deserted and boarded up. As he stopped the car, alongside the rough wooden picnic table in front of the first cabin, Branco turned to Michael.

"I told the owner the sheriff sent me," he said. "He let me have the cabin even though they're closed for the season."

Michael looked at the dilapidated shack.

"Let's hope we won't need it too long," he said.

They got out and walked toward it. Branco fished out a key and opened the door. It was a tiny, ten-by-fifteen, one-roomed affair, with two bunk beds, table and chairs, wardrobe, kitchen area with a little handbasin and small kerosene stove. Michael looked around. There was a single bulb dangling from the wire in the center of the ceiling and a lamp on the low table between the two beds.

Branco shut the door behind them. He walked over to the stove and opened a small brown paper sack that was standing on the top.

"I'll make some coffee," he said.

"What's the plan?" asked Michael, sitting in one of the chairs by the table.

"We must prepare," said Branco. "In the daytime, we'll look for him. At night, he looks for you. We must be ready."

As Branco got the coffee pot going on the stove, Michael crossed to one of the beds and sat down, testing the mattress.

"How?" he asked.

Branco pointed at him with a teaspoon.

"In this situation," he said, "weapons are useless. I have some wooden stakes in the car. I would like to show you how to use them."

"You know, Branco," Michael said, shaking his head slowly, "I don't think I've got the stomach for this sort of thing." He spread the fingers of one hand, palm upward in a kind of dumb plea for help. "I still find this whole business hard to believe," he said.

Branco looked at him sternly.

"When the time comes, you'll know exactly what to do," he said. The coffee pot was beginning to bubble on the stove. Branco strode over to the door. "I'll be right back," he said, going out.

Night had fallen. The sound of cicadas filtered through the still-open door. The moon was riding high and bright in a cloudless sky above the pines. Branco reached into the rear seat of the car and retrieved a bulky brown paper parcel. He tucked it under his arm and walked back into the cabin, closing the door behind him.

Branco dumped the parcel on the table and spread the wrappings wide. Inside lay a pile of round wooden stakes of uniform length. Every one had been sharpened to a fine point at one end. The inspector reached for the coffee pot from the stove, took out two mugs and began to pour it.

For the next few hours they talked, Branco doing most of the talking, delivering a condensed fireside version of one of his lectures on vampirism. He told Michael all the salient points about vampires: how the signs of their presence could be identified, how to track them down and how to classify and confirm their undead state.

Michael had never realized that the subject was so profuse and extensive and that vampirism had been and still could be spread so widely throughout the world. Finally, Branco dealt with the methods of disposal, concentrating on the use of wooden stakes and the precautionary necessity of cremation.

"You will not have time to make any mistakes," Branco said, summing up. For a moment, Michael had to suppress a snigger at the inspector's unintentional pun, but quickly saw that Branco was deadly serious.

"You must be swift and direct the point straight to the heart," Branco went on. "You must not hesitate."

He placed back on the table the stake he had been holding to illustrate his informal lecture and was about to reach for the coffee pot to fill up their mugs when a sound caught his ear.

There was a faint scratching at the door. Michael looked up.

"What's that?"

Branco held up a warning finger for silence.

"Don't move!" he breathed.

The scratching grew louder as they held their breath. Then another scratching began beneath one of the windows. Branco raised an eyebrow as Michael slowly got up from his chair. A third, distinctly different scratching started up from the wall behind the beds. Branco, looking gravely at Michael, picked up one of the wooden stakes from the table between them.

Michael looked questioningly at the detective when a low, rumbling growl emanated from the other side of the door.

"Sounds like dogs!" Branco hissed.

"Maybe they're mine!" Michael said, eagerly, and made a dash for the door. But Branco interceded, placing a hand on his chest. The growling outside grew louder and more fierce and a hefty thud shook the door. Next came an unnerving, unholy sound, half-groan, half-bark, the noise of no normal dog.

Branco shook his head.

"I doubt if they're yours," he said. He grabbed one of the wooden chairs and jammed it against the door, its back under the doorknob. The thudding against the door grew louder and more frequent, until the whole framework shook upon its hinges.

There was a loud crash of shattering glass and an enormous gray-and-black paw thrust through a window. They both started. Looking around, Branco quickly snatched up the coffee pot and hurled its boiling contents at the massive paw. A deafening howl of angry pain followed and the limb was withdrawn. Before the creature could try again, Michael grabbed one of the bunk beds and stood it on its end, jamming it hard against the splintered window. At that moment, the other window shattered and two giant paws appeared and, behind them, the ugly, snarling head of a dog, its lips wrenched back from two rows of misshapen fangs.

"Wolves!" Branco cried. But the light from the single bulb dangling from the ceiling was poor and, had he been able to look outside, the inspector would have seen quickly that, for once, he was wrong.

Buster and Annie—or at least, what they had become—were jumping up at the walls and windows of the cabin, raining mighty hammer blows on its sides with their paws and barking and snarling unceasingly. Zoltan was attacking the door, each time taking several paces back, then flying at it with the whole of his enormous weight behind each desperate lunge. The door's timbers sagged, but held. Zoltan howled ragingly at it, glanced up at the full moon, then threw back his head and howled again. The sound of the savage creatures' constant growling, barking, snarling and howling was becoming almost deafening to the two men inside the cabin. Zoltan ran around the back, where Buster was frantically clawing at the wall. He watched the other dog for a moment, then looked up and, with one mighty lunge of unearthly strength, bounded onto the roof in a single leap.

Balanced astride the apex of the roof, two feet on each of the sloping sides, Zoltan sniffed and scratched until he found a number of loose asphalt shingles. He began clawing and gouging at them furiously with his prodigious paws.

The three dogs were now attacking the cabin from three angles—front, rear and from above.

Inside, the two men looked worriedly all around them as the furious pounding, scratching and buffeting seemed to be going on from all directions, as if the very fabric of the whole building were being shaken and torn apart by an angry giant. For the moment, even the resourceful Inspector Branco was at a loss. He was unable to answer Michael's questioning look of fear as the cacophony of banshee howling and fearful, ghastly roaring went on deafeningly.

Zoltan was tearing away the asphalt shingles, and his great claws could be glimpsed from inside the shack, gouging furiously at the hardboard layers beneath, slashing them like paper.

Annie, who was at the window, had torn away part of the mattress from the bunk bed and was hurling herself at the bedframe, trying to push it inward.

The claws of Buster, rending at the wooden planks of the door, had begun to show through in places, little shreds of wood flaking off and falling to the floor inside. Frustrated at the lack of progress, the dog next began burrowing furiously beneath the door, trying to tunnel his way in. Within seconds, Michael could see the dog's paws, shoveling out scoops of earth below the door frame.

Powerless to do anything against the superhuman energies of the monstrous attackers outside, Branco and Michael slowly backed into corners of the shack, looking fearfully at each other as the onslaught continued. The roof shook wildly under the dreadful gouges of the beast up there, and the single light bulb swung erratically on its cord.

Both bunk beds were jammed against the windows, and one shook with the continuous blows of one of the dogs as if it were about to fall in. Michael crawled warily over and, putting his back against the frame of the bed, tried to hold it secure.

Branco glanced up to see that the creature on the roof had now made a large hole and he could see the ghastly face of Zoltan peering in. The dog had encountered a series of wires in the roofing and attacked them with his teeth. There were crackling sparks and a flash—and the single light bulb in the ceiling went out, plunging the cabin in total darkness.

Branco had a sudden idea. Getting up from his crouching position in the corner, he picked up two of the wooden stakes from the table. Throwing one over to Michael, he called out:

"Watch! Do as I do!" Branco felt his way over to the can of kerosene near the stove and dipped the end of his stake into it. Then he fished out a cigarette lighter and ignited it, holding it aloft like a torch. Michael proceeded to do the same.

The hole beneath the door was now large enough for a dog to put its head into. Annie's long snout peered into the cabin. Branco ran forward and jammed the flaming end of the improvised torch into the dog's face. There was a hideous shriek of pain and the animal leaped back. Michael went over to the window and, reaching over the torn mattress, thrust his torch into the face of Buster, who was about to stick his head into the room. The face disappeared and there was a horrible yelping sound.

Annie was rolling on the ground outside, screeching terribly, her face badly burned. Buster ran over to her, shaking his wounded head violently. Both dogs were wild with pain.

Up on the roof, Zoltan ceased his gouging

and tearing for a moment to peer down at the other two dogs. He bared his fangs and roared at them commandingly. The dogs looked up but barked defiantly, shaking their heads. Zoltan turned his fierce glare upon them, his eyes eyes like twin green search-lamps boring into their faces from his rooftop perch. He was using all his uncanny powers to try to get the two dogs to resume their attack on the cabin. But they did not obey. They retreated some distance from the cabin and waited, their fangs bared, watching silently.

Zoltan, with an angry snarl, went back to his desperate gouging at the roof shingles, trying to enlarge the hole he had made. His front paws pounded at the fabric like sledge-hammers.

Below, Branco and Michael looked up with dread at the increasing damage the beast was wreaking. The hut quivered and shook as a result of the savage efforts. Together, the men prepared two more stakes, dousing the ends in kerosene. Branco had his lighter at the ready as they gazed up fearfully at the shaking roof timbers.

Without warning, the whole framework, weakened by the terrible hammering it had suffered, groaned and caved in and the roof came crashing down. Branco and Michael did not have a chance to light their torches. They were buried under an avalanche of debris. Thudding down among all the rubble came the great hulk of Zoltan. He was flung sideways down a sloping section of the dismembered roof, crashing into the wall. He rolled over quickly and got to his feet, then threw back his head and howled with repulsive delight at his triumph.

He looked around, sniffing among the debris. Branco was beneath a pile of planks, unconscious. Veidt's words re-echoed in the malignant brain of the fiendish hound: "The only blood we need is the blood of Michael Drake."

Zoltan swung his gaze around. There, from beneath a pile of broken lath, plasterboard, and torn shingles protruded the legs of the victim he sought. Saliva dripping from his jaws, the huge dog approached, gloating with vile delight, and began to dig feverishly with his paws, tugging with his hungry fangs at heavy pieces of lumber in his haste to get at the throat of his master-to-be.

They are demons full of violence
Ceaselessly devouring blood.
Invoke the ban against them,
That they no more return to their neighbor-
   hood.
By Heaven be ye exorcised!
By Earth be ye exorcised!

—Ancient Babylonian fragment used
   against vampires

FIFTEEN:

Back to Base Camp

For twenty minutes or more the dog toiled on, slowly removing the rubble from Michael's body. Zoltan was gradually working toward his victim's neck, where he would perform his vile bloodletting rite. Grunting and gasping, his venomous jaws hanging open, the dog's amazing strength never seemed to flag. But even as he toiled, Zoltan became gradually aware of something happening; some change taking place in his surroundings that was of vital importance. He paused.

Through the jagged edges of what remained of the roof, the sky overhead was slowly growing lighter. Sunrise was approaching! Zoltan knew instinctively that he had to get back to the safety of his coffin before the first rays struck the valley. The other dogs, too, would have to crawl into the darkness of their burrows up on the hillside. Otherwise they would all be seared and blasted to agonizing oblivion by the sun's rays.

He looked down at his labors. He had come so close. . . . But it was too late to linger now. There would be other times, other opportunities. The main thing was to save himself. Drake might lie there injured for hours, perhaps even until nightfall when Zoltan would arise from his silent casket and return. With a snarl of impatience at being thwarted by nature, Zoltan looked up again at the sky. It *was* getting lighter.

He howled disdainfully, backing away from Michael's body. He climbed onto a pile of debris in the corner of the cabin and leaped up, clearing the confining wall in a single bound.

The two other vampire dogs were still outside waiting for him. As Zoltan landed nearby, they got up and the three dogs ran off through the woods, trying to beat the dawn back to the shelter of their custodian, Veidt Smit, and their daytime darkness.

Sheriff Larsen stepped out of the battered cabin after surveying the damage. It looked as if a tornado had torn it apart. Only the four walls remained standing. The door was clawed beyond repair and a hole had been gouged in the earth beneath it. Both windows were shattered, and inside the floor was still piled with the fallen wreckage of the roof and the splintered furniture.

He shook his head disbelievingly and walked over to the black Pontiac convertible parked several yards away. Branco and Michael were standing beside it. Both men were covered in dust and grime, their clothing was shredded, and they were bruised about the arms and faces.

Nearby, a deputy was sitting in the sheriff's car, talking on the radio.

"Those canyon dogs get hungry this time of the year, especially when there's no one around to feed 'em scraps," the sheriff said, as he came up to Branco and Michael. "But I've never seen it this bad before. I'll file a report today. . . . You sure you don't want me to drive you to the south end? There's a first-aid station there—"

"We're all right, thank you, Sheriff," Michael said. He rubbed his neck, massaging an aching muscle.

"Well," the sheriff said, "if you need me you know where I am."

"Thank you," Branco said.

The sheriff nodded and walked away. He got into the car with his deputy and drove off.

Michael looked after them, then turned to Branco.

"File a report!" he said. "They should get helicopters and capture those beasts before they kill someone."

Branco looked thoughtful. He still could not understand why the dogs had given up their attack after the roof fell in. He and Michael had been lying defenseless beneath the rubble for he didn't know how long, until the sheriff happened to drive by.

"You've been bothered by dogs since you started your vacation, isn't that what you told me?" he said.

"Yes . . . why do you ask?"

Branco patted Michael's arm.

"Let's go get some food and clean up," he said.

"Food?" Michael said. "Hell, I need a drink!"

"All right, a drink, too," the inspector agreed. They climbed into Branco's rented car, throwing their torn and dusty jackets in the back. They fell beside the small pile of wooden stakes which Branco had retrieved from the wreckage of the cabin.

"Mr. Drake," Branco said, starting the engine, "tonight, I want us to go back to your camping ground."

Michael looked at him increduously.

"Why?"

"I'm not sure," Branco said, stroking his

beard thoughtfully. He eased the car forward over the uneven terrain, toward the lakeside road. "But I have a feeling we might be closer there to what we're looking for," he added.

Michael could not help admiring the inspector's tenacity. He was at least twenty years Michael's senior, and yet, in spite of all that had happened during those terror-stricken hours in the cabin, ending with them being almost buried alive, here was Branco planning further schemes to track down his man. That notwithstanding the fact that those vicious wild dogs were still on the loose in the area.

It had been Branco, in fact, who had come to first under a pile of planks. He had managed to free himself from the rubble and then immediately set to work trying to dig out Michael, bringing him around with a handkerchief soaked in water from a nearby spring. It was then that the sheriff happened to drive up.

Had it not been for Branco's resourcefulness and quick-thinking action during their ordeal in the cabin—the scalding hot coffee, the chair jammed against the door, the improvised kerosene torches—those dogs might have got in and savaged them both.

By the time the two men reached a restaurant off the freeway, where they could freshen up in the washroom and have a drink and a meal, Michael had made up his mind. Whatever Branco was planning to do next, he would see him through it until the end.

Somewhere high overhead, probably on the tower, I heard the voice of the Count calling in his harsh, metallic whisper. His call seemed to be answered from far and wide by the howling of wolves. Before many minutes had passed a pack of them poured, like a pent-up dam when liberated, through the wide entrance into the courtyard.

There was no cry from the woman, and the howling of the wolves was but short. Before long they streamed away singly, licking their lips.

—Bram Stoker, *Dracula* (1897)
    (The New American Library, 1965)

SIXTEEN:

The Dogs Attack Again

Branco reached forward and took a pair of binoculars from the ledge beneath the car dashboard. Michael stood beside him and watched as the inspector slowly scanned around, down the lake, over to the woods on the far side, then up above to the hill beyond on the opposite shore. One side of the hill was a vertical earth bank like a small cliff

150

face. Branco stopped his panoramic sweep and stared intently. Up there near the summit of the hill, partially hidden in the trees, was a parked car. He looked more carefully, checking for any signs of activity. It was a long black vehicle . . . a hearse!

"See anything?" Michael asked.

"Not really," Branco lied and lowered his binoculars.

Branco's car was parked on the spot where Michael's camper had originally stood. In the back seat lay a newspaper package containing the wooden stakes and beside it, a wooden mallet.

Both men had cleaned up and changed and, after their meal, were feeling fresher, calmer and more alert.

Branco replaced the binoculars in the glove compartment, then reached in the back seat and opened the parcel. He took out two of the stakes and turned to Michael.

"Mr. Drake, it will be dark any moment," he said. "I'll look on that side of the hill." He pointed vaguely in the direction of the precipitous-faced hill across the lake where he had spotted the parked hearse. Michael nodded, watching his expression, wondering exactly what the inspector was up to. But he could read no hint of Branco's intentions.

"Uh . . . I'll go down by the lake," Michael said.

Confident that Drake was unlikely to be in any danger, Branco smiled reassuringly and set off toward the woods. Just before he disappeared into the trees, he turned and threw Michael a wave, almost as if he were simply setting off on a pleasant hike.

Michael stood by the car thoughtfully. He was still puzzled by the inspector's seeming lack of definite plans. Branco had seemed vague and evasive when Michael had asked him over the meal about his plans for that evening. And yet there was an air about Branco, a quiet confident manner that he knew precisely what he was looking for and that he would find it.

"Just keep on the alert," Branco had said simply. "Don't take any chances. And remember what I told you—weapons are no use. Only the stakes. Strike hard and accurately."

Could Branco have discovered, or deduced, or even guessed where Veidt Smit was hiding out? Michael wondered. Or perhaps the inspector was simply going to lie in wait somewhere in the woods, using Michael as bait out in the open, hoping that Smit would show himself.

He shrugged, took a stake from the back seat and wandered slowly down toward the lake, not quite certain what he was supposed to do.

The moon came up and rose steadily, large and clear over the valley, casting its sparkling phosphorescence off the lake, over the dull greenery of the trees, turning the distant mountains into ghostly cones of silver. The night was unnaturally silent.

Veidt Smit, from his high vantage point on the hill, had seen the familiar convertible below on the opposite side of the lake and the two men standing beside it, apparently conferring. It was time now to send the hell pack out to complete their work once and for all.

Zoltan sat before him attentively, Veidt's thought images forming in his diabolical brain. The master was angry and determined. This time there must be no mistakes, no unfinished business. There were only two men to be dealt with and they were both out there now in the open, defenseless. Zoltan was to take the other Hounds of Dracula—and strike swiftly.

His own target was to be Michael Drake. If necessary, the other dogs would deal with the second man. But Drake had to be secured at all costs, so that he would become their master. They were all, all of them, here only to serve.

Zoltan bared his fangs as if in acknowledgment that he understood.

"Go!" Veidt ordered. The dog sprang up and ran off down toward the embankment and into the trees, where, he knew, the others were waiting hungrily.

Inspector Branco finally neared the crest

of the hill where he had glimpsed the parked hearse. He stooped, stakes in one hand, and scooped up a largish stone that would serve as a hammer. He slipped it into his pocket.

Ahead lay a large clump of thick bushes. Stealthily, he skirted the edge of it and found himself in a small clearing. He looked around and there on the far side, partly in shadow, stood the black limousine, silent and ominous, symbol of all mortals' final one-way journey. He crept cautiously toward it and tried to peer through the frosted glass in the rear panels. A dark shape lay inside, but he could not make it out properly. He would have to move around to the front where the windows were of clear glass. He glanced up and down, making sure that he was not being observed, then moved slowly forward along the car. As he stalked past the front driver's door it was flung violently open, knocking him to the ground and sending the wooden stakes flying from his grasp.

Before he could move where he lay, the lithe figure of Veidt Smit dived out of the car and was on top of him, ice-cold hands clutching around his throat, squeezing with amazing strength. Branco felt his windpipe constricting and his eyes bulging painfully from their sockets, involuntarily flooding with tears at the pain. He tried to open his mouth, gasping for air. He could feel the grogginess increasing.

With the last-ditch, superhuman effort of

a desperate, dying man, he brought his knees swiftly up under Veidt's body, at the same time lunging upward with his fists at the arms angling down toward his neck. Smit, caught off guard, was somersaulted forward over the inspector's head, landing awkwardly with the side of his face to the ground, his limbs buckled under him.

Branco sprang up and threw a kick at the black figure, but Veidt swiftly rolled sideways with it and caught only a glancing blow in the ribs. The inspector quickly saw where the stakes had fallen and made a dive for them. But Smit was on his feet and booted him in the side of the head, knocking him away from them. Stunned, Branco tried to stagger to his feet, knowing that it was a grim fight that would end only in the death of one of them. Smit's foot lashed out again, smashing into his ribs. He fell over, gasping and retching, and Smit was quickly astride him, hands around his throat once more. Branco clawed frantically at the vise-like fingers, which were tightening on his windpipe. Deliberately, he made a gurgled choking sound and feigned unconsciousness, letting his body go limp and rolling back his eyes. The ploy worked. Veidt loosened his grip slightly and it gave Branco time to bring up the rock he had fumbled from out of his pocket and smash it against Veidt's temple as hard as he could. With a low moan, Veidt topped from him and lay still.

Branco struggled up quickly and dived again for one of the wooden stakes. Then he ran over to Veidt and, turning him over, knelt beside him. He raised the stake high above his head, grasping it with both hands like a sacrificial dagger. He took careful aim, then brought it down with all his might, plunging it into the heart of the semi-human being who bore the taint of vampirism. Being already unconscious, Veidt did not cry out, making the bloodcurdling shriek that Branco had heard all too many times before. There was simply a choking gurgle from the creature's throat, and a crimson stain spread rapidly around the stake on which he was impaled.

Branco, struggling breathlessly, grasped Veidt's body beneath the arms and dragged it to the hearse. He rolled it beneath the car at the rear, below the gas tank. He then went to the front and moments later returned with a spiked metal tool. With it he battered fiercely at the gas tank until it punctured and the gasoline poured out, drenching the body beneath it.

Branco took out his lighter, stepped backward, flicked it alight and prepared to throw it.

Michael was walking back from the edge of the lake to the convertible when he saw the great sheet of flame and the black smoke blanket rising from somewhere high on the hillside. He was about to turn and run toward it when out of the woods, running at full speed, came a pack of three dogs, heading straight for him.

He broke into a run and made it to the convertible within seconds. First, he switched on the engine, then punched the button on the dashboard that would raise the convertible top automatically. As it began to rise, he reached around the inside doors and pressed the switches that raised the electrically powered windows.

He glanced up. The three dogs were getting closer, headed by the huge black-and-gray one he had encountered before. The convertible top seemed to be rising agonizingly slowly, and he wondered whether it would fold over to connect with the top frame of the windscreen in time.

The dogs were dead ahead, running abreast. Michael reached forward and flicked on the headlight, high-beam. The blinding light momentarily blinded and startled the dogs. But after a second's hesitation which slowed them down, they broke formation and kept coming, streaking out of the headlamps' area.

All the time Michael was aware of the sluggish hum of the mechanism that powered the convertible top. He glanced up and saw the fabric hood moving forward so slowly he felt like grabbing it and forcing it forward into place.

On and on streaked the dogs, the sounds of their savage barking and snarling growing louder and louder. When the convertible top was still inches from the frame of the windshield, Michael noticed with horror that the dogs were almost within jumping distance of the car.

Zoltan seemed to fly through the air in a mighty leap to land on the hood of the car, his great bulk obscuring the whole windshield. Buster hurled himself up onto the roof and ran forward, managing to get one paw between the still-moving top and the top of the windshield.

Michael reached in the back seat, grabbed the mallet, swiveled and struck at the paw with pounding blows. The dog yelped deafeningly, withdrawing its injured paw. Michael grabbed the leading edge of the convertible top and hurriedly clamped it into place.

Through the front windscreen, his face in a hideous snarl of fury, Zoltan beat at the glass with his hammer-paws, barking and howling insanely. The dog on the roof began scratching fiercely at the fabric. Michael wondered how long it could hold, especially since he had seen these same animals virtually tear a wooden cabin apart.

Another dog's face appeared, blurringly at first, jumping at the driver's door. Michael turned, startled, and stared into its repulsive expression of utter hatred. Then, with a start, he realized—it was Annie, his own German shepherd! He was nauseated by the grisly change that had come over her, her face deformed and disfigured by the enlarged teeth and frightful fangs, her eyes staring wide and utterly malignant.

Michael turned away to see the first demonic hound, still on the hood before him. Its face was up hard against the glass and it was actually trying to bite or chew its way through, its jaws opening into a diabolical gaping black maw, then clamping shut again as they slipped ineffectively on the smooth surface. At that instant, with the dog crouching full-face to him, Michael's heart missed another beat. There flashed fleetingly into his mind a fragment of memory that had lurked vaguely in his subconscious but now blazed forth as absolute certainty: *he knew, without any doubt, that the fiend incarnate before him was the very same animal as the dog in the old daguerreotype that he had found among the photographs in the trunk in his garage.*

Stricken by the uncanny truth facing him, Michael released the brake, jammed the car into drive and hit the gas pedal. But the wet grass made the wheels spin wildly, throwing up chunks of earth, and instead of shooting forward suddenly as he had hoped, the car began to skid sideways in wide arcs. The dogs kept their hold, both the one on the hood and the other on the roof. Annie was still running beside the vehicle, barking wildly and making frantic lunges at the door.

Michael glanced upward to see that Buster, on the roof, had now succeeded in making a tear in the fabric. Desperately, he grasped the mallet with one free hand and beat at the paw that poked through. But it was difficult to control the car as it careened among the widely spaced trees at the edge of the wood, and each time he turned back to the wheel the paw resumed its vicious clawing and tearing. All the while, the dogs kept up their nerve-shattering, ear-splitting cacophony of howls, shrieks and yelps, lending the whole uproar the insane atmosphere of some tableau from the very abyss of hell itself.

Straining to try to see beyond the hulk of the dog blocking his view on the hood, Michael thought he glimpsed something ahead to the left, moving swiftly out of the woods toward him. He aimed directly at it and, as he drew nearer, saw to his amazement that it was Samson, streaking along and barking angrily.

He wrenched the wheel suddenly to the left, jamming on the brakes and going into a sharp broadside skid. Zoltan and Buster were flung from the hood and roof by the impetus and the car halted momentarily alongside Samson.

"Come, Samson! Quick!" Michael yelled,

leaning across to open the passenger door. "Quick! Jump in the back!"

The dog obediently leaped into the rear seat, while Michael slammed the door shut and locked it. He gunned the engine and took off toward the woods, trying to head for the dirt road leading to the freeway access road. Behind, he could hear the enraged barking of the three vampire dogs, hot in pursuit.

Out of breath, Michael shouted at Samson, keeping his eyes on the road ahead.

"Where have you been?" he yelled angrily.

Samson crouched on the seat directly behind him. Well, at least he had an ally now. But where the hell was Branco? He glanced in the rear-view mirror.

To his horror, there leering at him from behind was not Samson, but what once had been Samson. Like the others, his jaws were crammed with gigantic teeth and two long, curved fangs. The lips were peeled back in a permanent loathsome snarl, and the eyes burned with a sulfuric hostility. With a terrifying roar, the dog sprang forward, and Michael instinctively let go of the wheel, throwing up his arms to try to protect his head. The car veered out of control and, as Michael's foot came off the gas pedal as he struggled with the dog, came to an abrupt halt. The other three dogs outside were soon upon it again, gnawing, pounding and clawing in their renewed efforts to get in.

Meanwhile, Michael was having a terrible struggle with the powerful Samson, rolling and crashing about the interior of the car as his former pet tried to tear at him with his savage fangs. He punched and kicked at the animal's head, landing pounding blows and at the same time writhing and squirming convulsively in his attempts to escape being bitten. He felt his flesh being lacerated and his clothing being torn, the dog's muscular limbs lashing and kicking in a dreadful frenzy.

They struggled over the seats and, stretching out an arm, Michael grasped one of the wooden stakes from the rear. Heaving with his shoulder, he managed to throw the dog off balance, head first over the seat. Then, as it lunged at his leg, he brought the stake down with both hands into Samson's chest. The animal gave out a loud, agonized moan and a choking death rattle, horrifying to hear, came from its throat. The sound even momentarily silenced the uproar of the other three beasts outside.

Then the terrible, unearthly pandemonium began once more. It seemed to Michael to have been going on for hours, but in fact it had only been in progress for something over ten minutes. The eldritch sounds had, however, echoed and carried across the moonlit lake valley, bringing Branco, exhausted as he was from his struggle with Smit, racing down through the woods from the hillside.

From another direction, also attracted by the unbelievable din, Jo Jo and Sim, the fishermen, were hurrying along, carrying a rope and a rifle.

But Zoltan, now back on the car hood, seemed in imminent danger of smashing the windshield as he butted it with his bucket-sized head. Any minute now, Michael thought, as he heaved Samson's body to the floor, the gigantic obscenity would be upon him. He heard a loud tear from above and looked up to see that Buster had ripped a larger gash in the convertible top.

Jo Jo ran out of the brush and paused only a few feet from the car, aiming his rifle at the dogs. First he blasted at Buster on the roof, but although he saw with his own eyes the bullet tearing into the dog's side, it seemed to have no effect on the creature at all. He fired at Zoltan, a direct hit in the spine, between the shoulders, yet the brute did not even flinch. Then Annie took a bullet. But she too continued battering at the car as if nothing had happened.

Incredulous, Jo Jo and Sim gazed wide-eyed at each other. They were about to move in closer when a shout rang out from the woods behind them. Branco was heading toward them, running as fast as he could, still clutching the second of the two wooden stakes he had taken from the car.

Suddenly, Buster leaped down from the roof of the car, hurling himself at Jo Jo. Sim jumped astride the animal as it landed and whipped a length of rope around its throat, yanking with all his might, garroting the creature as it struggled beneath him, its head wrenched backward. Seeing the danger to her companion, Annie launched herself at Jo Jo and he swung the butt of his rifle like a club at her head, trying to fend her off.

Buster suddenly went limp beneath Sim, and he let the dog slump to the ground. Branco, rushing over with his stake, drove it viciously into the dog's heart as Sim stood by, horrified in the realization that this had once been his own dog.

There was a sickening crunch beside them as Jo Jo's rifle butt connected, stoving in the side of Annie's skull. The great German shepherd staggered and fell to the ground unconscious.

Zoltan, bellowing with rage as he rammed his head repeatedly against the windshield, suddenly became aware that he was battling on alone. He stopped and looked around.

Branco was crouching beside the driver's door, calling to Michael inside.

"Quick! A stake!"

Swiftly, Michael grabbed one from the rear seat and thrust it out through the torn convertible top. The inspector snatched it and ran over to the stunned form of Annie— and performed the same gruesome ritual with which he had dealt with Buster as the two fishermen looked on, disbelievingly.

Zoltan roared with anger as he saw that his two vampire-dog companions were slain. The three men nearby froze, wondering which one of them the largest, fiercest hellhound of all would attack first. But instead, Zoltan leaped from the hood of the car and streaked off toward the forest without even looking their way.

Michael restarted the car and flung it forward, in pursuit of the fleeing monster. Zoltan made the cover of the trees quickly, but Michael hit the brakes, grabbed up the mallet and a stake and jumped out to continue after him on foot.

Ahead he could see the shadowy movement of the creature, bounding up a slope. Michael kept on, running like a maniac. Zoltan reached the summit of the hill ahead of him, turned and sat on his haunches, waiting. Within seconds, his pursuer appeared over the brow of the hill, marching determinedly toward him, stake and mallet at the ready. Michael halted only three feet away, glaring with absolute hatred at the satanic, gloating thing before him.

He was about to take another step forward when the dog's eyes caught his gaze. They seemed to glow, pulsing with a malign, yet fascinating brimstone hue. Michael stared unblinkingly, not realizing that he was becoming mesmerized by the dog's infernal, hypnotic glare. The eyes grew larger and larger until they were all that he seemed able to see. Some barbarous, devilish power stabbed into his brain, alien and awesomely paralyzing. He felt dizzy. His tense muscles relaxed. The hands went limp. The stake and mallet dropped to the ground. He stood there, utterly defenseless.

Zoltan crouched, ready to pounce, keeping his powerful gaze upon the man before him. Michael could see the dog plainly now, its great fanged jaws slavering obscenely. He knew something was wrong; knew the beast was about to spring, but felt strangely resigned to the fact, unable to do anything, like someone trying vainly to awaken from a horrific nightmare. He struggled mentally, trying to gather all his resources into one powerful spiritual effort. A bright symbol darted fleetingly into his mind for a split second, bathing him with light.

And he suddenly knew what he must do. With all his might he willed himself to act. Slowly, he raised his arms to his chest and pulled open his shirt, the buttons popping off as he did so. There, gleaming on his chest, dangling on its chain, was the silver crucifix he always wore.

Zoltan's eyes rolled wide and he tried to turn his head in a convulsive stricture, away from the shining cross. He opened his throat in a ghastly, nerve-jarring scream of pain and horror and began to edge slowly backward. The eerie, compelling light had died from his eyes.

As if the noise had triggered some inner mechanism, Michael was entirely himself again. He knew he had one powerful protection against the drooling, demented parody of an animal that confronted him.

The dog growled, insane with fury, as Michael advanced, still displaying the cross. Then suddenly it stumbled backward and disappeared from sight. A split second later the most horrendous, drawn-out shriek of agony scythed out across the valley.

Holding the cross before him, Michael stepped forward and found himself on the edge of the sheer drop down the side of the high hill.

Below lay the hulk of Zoltan, impaled through the chest on one of the sharp-pointed wooden palings that lined the private property on the lakeside embankment. The vampire dog was still staring up at him as he peered over the edge.

Then, with an agonized groan, the obscene blasphemy heaved its final breath; its head sagged and its foul swathe of a tongue lolled out from between the limp jaws.

Michael stood, still holding his crucifix, trying to catch his breath as the perspiration soaked his face and body.

Branco and the two fishermen stood by the torn convertible and the staked bodies of Buster and Annie as Michael staggered unsteadily out of the nearby woods. The inspector noted the look of utter exhaustion on Drake's face.

"Are you all right?" he asked.

Michael came up to him and sighed heavily.

"The dog is dead," he said simply.

"Are you sure?"

"I'm sure."

"The inspector here's been telling us some pretty tall stories," Jo Jo said, grinning.

"Yeah. Hard to swallow," said Sim.

Michael looked wearily from one to the other.

"Believe me, gentlemen," he said, "everything Inspector Branco told you is true." He looked at Branco. "Thank God it's all over."

"What'll we do with the dead animals?" Sim asked the Inspector.

"Burn them," Branco said. "*All* of them. And after we burn them, we will scatter their ashes in the wind."

He turned to Michael and placed a hand on his shoulder.

"You can go home now, Mr. Drake," he said. "That was the last of them."

"Thank God," Michael said.

Epilogue

The lakeside camping grounds were deserted. Winter was approaching. There was no evidence of the scenes of horror and violence that had occurred at Lake Arrowhead toward the end of the summer. The water lapped gently at the shores and the trees waved their branches lazily in the chilly breeze. Only the moon surveyed the valley where the Hounds of Dracula had terrorized Michael Drake and his family.

By the lakeside the gnarled old tree looked grotesque in the half-light. Beneath it, leading into the undergrowth, lay a trail of small, torn, dead things: a lapwing, a squirrel, a shrew, a rabbit, a young otter. Little sad, still bundles of bloodied fur and feathers. Had anyone seen them he would have guessed that a polecat was on the prowl. The trail led to a small burrow in an earthen bank beneath the trees. Out of it into the moonlight came a small, sturdy shape. It raised its head and its eyes gave off a baleful glint of jade green in the moonlight. Then it drew back its lips from a row of horrid fangs, still dripping with blood and gore. Then what had once been Annie's cuddly, furry little puppy put back his head and howled at the night. . . .